Count Luna

ALEXANDER
LERNET-HOLENIA

Count Luna

translated from the German
by Jane B. Greene

A NEW DIRECTIONS PAPERBOOK

Originally published as *Der Graf Luna* by Paul Zsolnay Verlag, Vienna, Austria. This edition is published by arrangement with Adelphi Edizioni and the heirs of Alexander Lernet-Holenia.

Manufactured in the United States of America
First published as a New Directions Paperbook (NDP1483 in 2020)

Library of Congress Cataloging-in-Publication Data
Names: Lernet-Holenia, Alexander, 1897–1976, author. | Greene, Jane Dannard, translator.
Title: Count Luna / Alexander Lernet-Holenia ; translated from the German by Jane B. Greene.
Other titles: Graf Luna. English
Description: First New Directions edition. |
New York : New Directions Publishing, 2020.
Identifiers: LCCN 2020012652 | ISBN 9780811229616 (paperback) | ISBN 9780811229623 (ebook)
Subjects: LCSH: Revenge—Fiction. | Paranoia—Fiction.
Classification: LCC PT2623.E74 G713 2020 | DDC 833/.912—dc23
LC record available at https://lccn.loc.gov/2020012652

10 9 8 7 6 5 4 3 2 1

New Directions Books are published for James Laughlin
by New Directions Publishing Corporation
80 Eighth Avenue, New York 10011

Count Luna

Chapter 1

On Thursday, May 6 of last year, a man by the name of Alexander Jessiersky arrived in Rome and took a room in a hotel on the Piazza di Spagna. He registered as an Austrian citizen, born in 1911, and a widower. His occupation he did not fill in, perhaps because he did not know how to translate it into Italian.

On the morning of the seventh, he booked passage on the *Aosta*, which was to sail for Buenos Aires from Naples on the evening of the ninth.

In the afternoon of the seventh, he visited various places of interest in the southern sections of Rome, including the Appian Way. Either at the Church of Domine Quo Vadis or at the nearby Temple of the Deus Rediculus—one dedicated to the Christian, the other to the pagan, deity of return—he would have done well to have taken the hint and turned back. But, unfortunately, he did not do so. He went on to the Church of Sant'Urbano, which contains a side entrance to the Catacombs of St. Praetextatus.

While looking around the church, he asked the custodian whether it was true that some time before, two French priests had entered the catacombs from the church and had never returned. The custodian replied in the affirmative; whereupon Jessiersky remarked that he planned to come back the next day and go down into the catacomb to search for the vanished priests. Jessiersky's Italian was not of the best, but the custodian managed to get the drift of what he was saying. He told Jessiersky that he himself was not authorized to conduct him into the catacombs, nor would anyone else be willing to do so. These catacombs, he explained, were for the most part unexplored, which was doubtless why the two priests had lost their way and perished. The visitor would, therefore, do better to remain in the church looking at its famous frescoes. Jessiersky replied that he did not want a guide and would be able to find his way by himself. The custodian pointed out that by now the bodies of the two lost men must certainly be in a state of advanced decomposition, but Jessiersky cut short this and other objections with a generous tip.

The next day he came back equipped with candles, a suitcase, and a light coat and, ignoring the renewed protests of the custodian, crawled through the entrance to the catacombs beneath the altar of the lower church, pulled suitcase and coat in after him, and, like the two priests, was never seen again.

The custodian waited until evening, then he sent out an alarm to the personnel of the nearby Catacombs of St. Sebastian. The personnel heaped reproaches upon him for having permitted the foreigner to enter the catacombs at all and set out at once to look for the missing man.

All attempts to find him proved unsuccessful, including the search instituted by the police and directed and supervised with the greatest care by Professors F. B. Degrassi and Innocente Bazzi, eminent authorities on subterranean Rome. It was not even possible to distinguish Jessiersky's footprints on the dusty floors of the passageways from those of others who had been there before him. The Catacombs of St. Praetextatus, like those of St. Sebastian, of St. Calixtus, and of Domitilla, comprise, in addition to the familiar passages through which visitors are conducted every day, a maze of further passages, not entered for a very long time and said to be connected with the passages, galleries, and tomb chapels of those other catacombs that form a wide arc about the city of Rome; the foreigner could very easily have lost his way and died of starvation.

As is well known, the Italian catacombs, and the Roman ones in particular, were the burial places of the first Christians. The word is Greek and originally denoted a receptacle hollowed out of a hill, in other words a sand or tufa pit, into which the corpses of slaves and criminals were thrown after they had been worked to death. But even in very early times the bodies of martyrs were put into these often quite inaccessible cavities (then called crypts) to prevent their venerated remains from falling into the hands of the pagans. And since it was the wish of many Christians to be buried near a martyr because they hoped that the body of a saint would give some protection to their own bodies, these places were gradually extended to form entire underground grave-yards, or *coemeteria*. On the anniversaries of the martyrs' deaths, the congregation would assemble there to hear mass and receive communion. In times of persecution, Christians would take refuge in the *coemeteria*, although they were, all too often, pursued even under the earth, and many of them met death in the realm of the dead.

The structure of the Roman catacombs is in itself very simple. It consists of narrow passages, the lateral walls of which are lined with several tiers of hollow niches, one above another, designed to receive the bodies. Tablets of marble or terra cotta, bearing inscriptions, close up the niches. But with more and more dead to be interred, more and more passages had to be excavated, and thus there came into being those many-storied, labyrinthine structures that even in ancient times made it increasingly difficult for the brotherhoods responsible for the care of the necropolises, the so-called *Fossores* and *Innocentiores*, to find their way.

Then came the end of the persecutions and the establishment

of Christianity as the state religion. The underground worship was transferred to the churches above ground, and the new custom was introduced of burying the dead in and around these churches. From the time of Pope Paul I, the remains of most of the martyrs were removed to the Pantheon or other worthy places in the city itself. As the catacombs themselves lost their importance, the knowledge of their construction was soon forgotten. During the Middle Ages, only the Catacombs of St. Calixtus were visited by the faithful, and it was not until the beginning of modern times that people became again interested in the other burrows of the first Christians. Until late in the nineteenth century, large sections of the catacombs were no longer visited. Even today, in fact, there are some that have never been explored.

Nevertheless, many capable scholars have attempted to map out sizable sections of that sinister and dangerous underworld of Rome, which is plunged in eternal darkness. Largely because of the many-storied construction and because of the caving-in of so many parts, those scholars found themselves confronted with considerable difficulties. In some instances, though not in all, they have coped with the problem very ingeniously, and now the question was raised as to whether the vanished foreigner might have carried one of these maps with him, that of Savinio, perhaps, or of Boccalini. For if he had such a map, it might yet serve to lead him to safety. But the custodian of Sant'Urbano was unable to give any information on that point.

The possibility that the foreigner might have left the catacombs at a place other than that at which he had entered was also explored. The regular entrance to the Praetextatus catacombs was not in Sant'Urbano, but at some distance from the church, in a sand pit, one of the so-called *arenariae*, dating from antiquity. But it was considered quite improbable that Jessiersky had found his way back to the light of day there or elsewhere. For had he done so, although he might not have felt obliged to inform the custodian, he would have returned to his hotel where he had left all his belongings and where his room was urgently needed for the accommodation of a high official who had arrived with his entire staff. Jessiersky, however, had not reappeared at the hotel.

Finally, there was the possibility that he might have taken along sufficient food to enable him to exist for a time under the earth. But the supply could not have been a very large one under any circumstances. Furthermore, the police had by now discovered that on the seventh he had reserved a passage on the *Aosta*, which had sailed from Naples for Buenos Aires on the ninth. The ship had left without him, and the cabin reserved for him had not been occupied.

So there was no alternative but to give him up for lost, to assume that yet another dead man had been added to the ranks of the ancient dead, and to call a halt to the investigations which had continued almost up to Ascension Day. As a precaution, however, though a somewhat belated one, the entrance under the altar of the lower church of Sant'Urbano, through which three persons had already vanished, was walled up.

In the course of the investigation, certain inquiries had brought out the fact that the last of these persons had been connected with some other incidents which had attracted notice in his own country, and in which its police were still interested.

The Austrian Ministry of the Interior, therefore, requested the Ministry of Foreign Affairs, through its diplomatic representatives in Rome, to urge the Italian authorities to look once again into the particulars of Jessiersky's disappearance. In addition, the Vienna authorities proceeded to do some research of their own into the history of the vanished man. Concerning this, as well as the events in Italy, Dr. Julius Gambs, of the Ministry of the Interior, drew up a comprehensive report. It is upon this report and upon various facts we ourselves have uncovered that we have based the following account of the extraordinary happenings that led to Jessiersky's disappearance.

Chapter 2

Around 1806, Pavel, the son of a certain Alexander Jezierskij, a native of Little Russia, settled in East Galicia in order to assume possession of the estates of his wife, the widow Raczynska, née Szoldrska. An impecunious army officer, he had met the Raczynski family during the campaign of 1805 when his contingent was stationed for a considerable time in Volhynia. Having made the acquaintance of the widow Raczynska, Pavel Alexandrovich Jezierskij allowed the troops to continue on their way west without him and thus failed to witness the meeting of the Russian and Austrian armies and the famous sunburst of Austerlitz on December 2 of that year. Instead, he asked to be retired from active service, began to court, and soon married the widow. He then established himself solidly in Wiazownika and Marianowka, the two estates that had been her dowry in her first marriage, and shortly thereafter was accepted into the Polish nobility and given the Ciolek coat of arms. But as this acceptance had taken place at a time when the Grand Duchy of Warsaw was under French protection, the Austrian Empire, when it regained possession of Galicia, stubbornly refused to take notice of the Jezierskij nobility.

When Pavel Jezierskij's wife died—and she died very soon—he immediately remarried, this time one of his old sweethearts from Russia, the daughter of a man by the name of Bielski, the Starost of Utaikov, who claimed to be a prince. With this second bride, an extravagant lady, he squandered the dowry of his first, more frugal wife. Of Marianowka and Wiazownika, Olgerd, his son by the widow Raczynska, was never to see so much as a blade of grass. Pavel Jezierskij himself had no choice but to give up his life as the proprietor of an estate and become a lawyer in Lemberg. But in that profession, he had little success. He plunged further and further into debt, and after a last attempt to squeeze some money out of Slobodka, an estate in the Stryi District that he still owned though it was leased, he died a ruined man. Because of this, one of his sons, Witold, born in 1837, was compelled to stoop to paid espionage, in the interests of the country of his fathers and to the detriment of his own. His activities were exposed, but not entirely. For Witold had been careful not to commit his misdemeanors alone and managed to implicate several of his colleagues in the gubernatorial government. As a result, his highest superiors, Vice-President von Kalchberg and Councillor von Mosch, instead of creating a scandal which would have brought disgrace not only upon half of the government of Galicia, but also upon themselves, hushed up the affair and simply ordered the immediate removal of those of their subordinates who had been directly involved.

So Witold Jezierskij went to Trieste where he tried in a different way to rise again in the world. First he asked to be allowed to spell his name "Jessiersky," because it looked less Russian. And his request, regarded as only right and reasonable in the light of past events, was granted. He then applied for permission to assume the name of his mother and to call himself "Jessiersky-Bielsky," which, to be sure, sounded quite Russian. Since, however, it might also be Czech and since that second request was considered a matter of minor consequence anyway, the authorities acceded to it. But when, obviously in pursuance of a long-deliberated plan, he also petitioned for the official recognition of the Polish knighthood, he received a curt refusal. With this failure, all further projects he might have entertained, such as getting himself elevated to the rank of a Prince Bielsky, went up in smoke.

In dejection, he married Sophie von Grabaricz, the quite penniless daughter of a naval officer. He had two children by her, a son, whom he put into military school, and a daughter. This poor creature, because he was persuaded that no one would marry her and because she could speak a few words of Polish, he prevailed upon to enter the Convent of the Barefoot Carmelites in Cracow.

The son, Adam Jessiersky, served first in the infantry and later on the general staff. In 1908, by then a captain, he married a Fräulein Fries.

Gabriele Fries came of a very wealthy family. Her father owned a big transport business, the former Strattmann Palace in Vienna at 8 Bankgasse, and the Zinkeneck estate in the Alps. He had two sons, and when the war broke out in 1914, he did everything in his power to prevent them from being slaughtered on the altar of the fatherland. His son-in-law, however, who meanwhile had been promoted to the rank of major, was no less active in his endeavors to bring about the precise opposite. As a result of his military connections, he was successful. Working officially for, unofficially against, the family, he managed not only to get the two young men drafted but also to have them sent to the front. What is more, he had all the good fortune he had been hoping for. Both sons fell in battle and the entire Fries fortune was designated to go to his wife.

He himself, of course, did not fall. He reached a colonel's rank and lived until 1925, when he died of cancer.

He left one son, named Alexander after the first Jezierskij about whom anything was known, but also in memory of all the other ancestors whose existence could only be surmised, the felt-clad Russian horsemen.

The relationship between this child and his progenitor was not of the best. It would be going too far to assume that the child, for all his precociousness, could actually have known so early how ungentlemanly, how ruthlessly ambitious certain officers can be. Moreover, Adam Jessiersky was very clever at acting the polished gentleman. He was well-built and his hands were beautiful, especially when, at a social gathering or at the theater, they rested on his saber hilt. He wore an air of composure, never betraying his inner state, which was anything but composed. There was an aura of mystery about him, of something not quite reputable in his past, which lent him a peculiar kind of attraction. Although he had not been granted nobility, he knew how to behave as though he were noble nonetheless, and as though at any moment he might come into an estate or inherit a castle in Galicia. Rumor had it that he deceived his wife. No one doubted for an instant that he was quite capable of following in his father's footsteps and spying for the Russians. In reality, of course, as the son-in-law of the wealthy Fries, he had not the slightest need to do anything of the sort. On the contrary, he was the most conscientious of army men and had even sacrificed his own brothers-in-law to the fatherland!

But nevertheless, his son, even as a child, found this fellow who was his father nothing short of loathsome. Nor did he have any real affection for his mother, although she was unhappy with her husband. She was too inept to find happiness with other men. Old Fries, too, with his businessman's ways and his habit, probably dating from the days of detachable cuffs, of pushing up his shirt cuffs, and his mourning for his fallen sons, was decidedly boring to his grandson. So it might well be asked whom the child did love. He loved no one. He was one of those children who very early become aware that they exist only for themselves. Alexander Jessiersky would have got along with that other Alexander, the father of Pavel, the ancestor of this whole questionable race, far better than with his own father.

In short, the two Jessierskys were disquieting foreign elements in the Fries family, all the more so because, as is frequently the case with exotic gentlemen, they did not get along with each other. That Adam Jessiersky had, for his part, begun to feel an aversion for his son became evident in the last years of his life, particularly when he took a hand in the boy's education.

When he came into the nursery for this purpose, he would drop heavily into the most comfortable chair and cross his legs, and the chair would give a loud crack. The child was annoyed by that cracking of the chair under the weight of his father who, though a handsome man, in recent years put on weight. He also felt an intense dislike for the crossing of those shapely legs. For, although the colonel had for a long time worn civilian clothes, they somehow seemed still to be cased in military breeches. What annoyed Alexander was that his father's robust thighs were so much in evidence in this position. It disturbed the boy because, although he knew very well that at the beginning of his career his father had marched on foot at the head of an infantry company and later sat around at various General Staff desks, his son could not dispel the notion that this overdeveloped bottom was the result of a great deal of riding, of a continual grinding, rubbing, and kneading of the horse beneath the colonel. Furthermore, Adam Jessiersky—so his son could not help imagining—had on occasion not merely followed some general out to the Vienna parade ground on horseback, but regularly galloped over the undulating hills of Poland at the head of thundering squadrons of uhlans. Like the general staff, the uhlans wore dark green uniforms—dark green tunics with red facings and with golden cords dangling from the officers' shoulders. The lances in the front ranks swayed in the wind like spikes of wheat, the small black and yellow pennons fluttering gaily. To accompany that spectacle, Chopin himself—whose music little Alexander had to practice on the piano—seemed to play his wild, revolutionary fantasies. There was always some sort of insurrection seething beneath the surface among those outwardly tamed Poles.

With his beautiful beringed hand, which always seemed to emerge from the narrow sleeve of an uhlan's tunic, Alexander's father would reach for a textbook and begin to examine him. Where on earth had the colonel picked up this indescribably nonchalant gesture? Perhaps he had copied it from some archduke, while serving as a member of the suite, for he always displayed an unusual aptitude for imitating the manners of those above him and also for inducing people who would otherwise never have thought of entering his house to associate with him.

The colonel was the product of a no longer wholly comprehensible past. Perhaps to compensate for this fact, he prided himself on being a child of his own age. He believed that it was of the utmost importance to master such sciences as mathematics, geography, or physics. Disciplines, such as literature or the fine arts, he deemed useful only to the extent that they would, say, enable an officer to compose a patriotic speech, or see that the birthday banquet for a superior was properly laid by the mess orderlies. Concerning philosophy and religion, he preserved a discreet silence. He liked to put in an appearance at the so-called Society Mass and to see who was there. But he considered superstition more useful than any faith, and the Devil figured far more prominently in his conversation than his own Maker.

His son, however, for some reason, had already gone far beyond this kind of thinking. He felt that instead of becoming enmeshed in the material world, one should leave it to those who were already enmeshed in it, like old Fries, for example, and his employees, so that one could lead one's own life. Where Brussels was situated and what sort of goods were consumed there was, after all, of no importance; moreover, once you had learned about Brussels, you had to find out about Bucharest or Oslo, and so forth. And while it might be important for a bookkeeper to be able to do arithmetic, what need was there for his father to examine *him* in arithmetic? To a large number of questions, and often quite deliberately, in fact, the son gave no answer. But when his father, who had an excellent command of French, made French conversation, and his son did not reply like a Parisian, a violent quarrel would break out in the nursery, and the colonel would lay the responsibility for the boy's apparent lack of talent squarely at the door of the Fries family. For old Fries and his daughter Gabriele spoke French with what might be described as bourgeois coyness. In reality, however, the son spoke French poorly only because his father wanted him to speak it fluently and without an accent; and as time went on, the son spoke worse and worse French until finally, with a nonchalant wave of his hand, Adam Jessiersky gave him up. He rose from his chair, thereby causing it to crack loudly once again, and, with an air of insulting indifference, left the room. There was absolutely nothing to be done, he implied, with the young people of the present who were so puny physically and mentally. Nor could anything better be expected in the future.

Adam Jessiersky's stoutness came to a sudden end when he fell ill with cancer. He grew exceedingly thin, then terrifyingly thin, and if children were able to feel pity, which, however, they are not, his son could not have helped pitying his father although he did not like him. But he did not pity him. Another emotion took possession of him. The more the father's illness increased, the more firmly did the notion become entrenched in the mind of the son that it was not really a disease, but a pretext. His father, the boy thought, was quite deliberately withdrawing into himself in order later on to join his ancestors who were far superior to the Fries family with whom he had been thrown. Then at last he would be able to live where he belonged—in a place from which the son, along with his mother and his grandfather, were and would forever be excluded.

The son, fourteen years old at that time, had even then gathered that the Jessierskys had been disreputable; he no longer had any illusions regarding his family. But whether they had been disreputable or not, or perhaps just because they had been, he felt that the family extended down as far as his father but not to him, the son! Between this father and this son something the two were unaware, or scarcely aware, of had taken place, and as a result, the son no longer belonged to his father. That estrangement in itself did not matter to the boy. In fact, it gave him great satisfaction. But because of it, he no longer belonged to his father's, that is, to his own, ancestors, and this, inexplicably, saddened him. He might tell himself a hundred times that they had been shady, in fact, downright corrupt, men   their fortune-hunting, their rascality, and perfidiousness did not make up to him for the fact that they had, as he firmly believed, rejected him. How, being dead, they had managed to do this, and why they had done it, he did not know.

Adam Jessiersky, however, who still belonged to them, now readied himself to return to them; and to the son it was as though the hearse would be taking his father not to the Trieste cemetery, but to Poland, or perhaps Russia. At his death, the colonel, disgusted with his son, with the Fries family, and possibly even with the general staff, would make preparations for the journey back to his true home. That, at least in his particular case, was the meaning of death.

Gabriele Jessiersky, who was still hopelessly in love with her husband, was with him day and night. Old Fries shoved up his shirt cuffs, wrung his hands, and went about bemoaning the fact that now, in addition to his two sons, he was about to lose his son-in-law. But all that seemed ridiculous and insignificant in comparison with Adam Jessiersky's death itself. When it came, this man, who had had so little to recommend him in life, displayed greatness in his manner of dying. The boy was very well aware of this, and the dying man also seemed to sense it. He was conscious of it and felt obligated to carry through with it.

The colonel's hands had become extremely emaciated. As they lay on the coverlet, they seemed made of transparent alabaster like the hands of a corpse. His feeble head, resting against the pillows, looked astoundingly aristocratic. It might have been assumed that this member of the general staff, who had sent so many to their death in order to escape it himself, would die without dignity. But he died with a dignity which was, to say the least, far more than merely military.

He had already lost consciousness when a priest appeared to perform the last offices, one of which was to anoint his feet for the road to eternity. When the covers were pulled back, it was revealed that the once shapely legs were now frightfully wasted.

They were quite unfit to carry him to his destination. But actually he would not have to go on foot like any peasant or tramp. He would be driven. And he would not have to depend on the hearse either! For the dead Jessierskys or even the Bielskis—having forgotten their annoyance with him because, like his father, he had annexed their name—would certainly send a carriage or a sleigh for him from the Beyond. And the Galician half bloods, by which the sleigh was drawn, with their ornamented head gear jingling and fluttering in the wind, would dash away with him into Eternity.

When Alexander Jessiersky thought back later on this death, it always seemed to him that his father, despite all the ill-feeling between them, ought to have told him how he had managed to die like that. But his father had died without telling him.

For months, even years, an unusually long time, at any rate, for a boy, he thought about his father's death. And instead of feeling relieved, as might have been expected in view of the uncomfortable relationship between them, he felt lonely and forsaken. He had never been to Poland, but now in his imagination he pictured a fantastic Poland, a kind of Beyond, in which the dead Jessierskys dwelt and from which the death sleigh had been sent. Beneath a gray sky, from which snow never fell but which held the constant threat of snow, there were always gay parties on the estates where the departed lived in death. Often the ghostly festivities would go on all night and into the next day, which would dawn as gray as the preceding one over the endless landscape with its blanket of old snow.

To the dreamer, translating space into time, this endlessness of the landscape seemed like eternity. But he, the dreamer, had not been invited to share this eternal life and would probably never be. Never would he drive, in one of those sleighs drawn by Galician half bloods, up to the door at Dobrovlany or Borek Stary, or whatever the estates were called, his feet in a fur bag, leaning back against a robe of twenty fox pelts, with the twenty sewn-on tails flapping about him in the wind. The Szoldrskis and Bielskis, the Przezdziekis and the Koscielez-Dzialynskis would wait for him in vain. Or rather they would not wait for him at all, for they had not invited him, still less had it occurred to the Jessierskys themselves to invite their descendant. In fact, the curious thing about this Eternity was that it was not God who sent people there, but the deceased themselves who decided who was to be allowed to enter and who was not. Like the wolves, of which there were still many in Poland, which would not permit the wolfhounds to approach them, though they were descended from them, these wolfish dead bit off their descendants. This was true not only of the Jessierskys, who after all came from the wolves' country, Russia, but also of their more civilized Polish relatives.

However, to the brooding boy, the only really savage, as it were, rapacious dead were the Jessierskys, and he began to deplore the fact that nothing was known about them before the Alexander Jezierskij he himself had been named for. Already the outlines of this same ancestor, whose patronymic had been forgotten, had become blurred in the twilight of the past, scarcely distinguishable from the background of his dead forebears. And farther back in the dusk were still more obscure ancestors. They were not standing in single file, like people waiting for a descendant to be born to them so that they themselves, in a way, might be able to go on existing. They were spread out like an open fan, growing dimmer and dimmer, and vanishing in all directions of oblivion; and the distance, which in Austria would have been scarcely two or three centuries away, was boundless in Russia and made them seem infinitely alien to the boy.

Alexander Jessiersky felt very much forsaken when the last real Jessiersky had departed, and it may well have been this feeling which led him to marry so early. At twenty-four he married a Baroness Pilas, who brought him as her dowry the estates of Hradek and Sossnowetz in Bohemia (1550 acres in all). But like Pavel Alexandrovich, who had squandered the property of his wife, Alexander Jessiersky was also unable to retain his wife's dowry: when the Czechoslovakian People's Republic took over all private property in 1948, the land was confiscated without compensation.

When Alexander Jessiersky married, his mother, Gabriele, née Fries, was still living in the former Strattmann Palace in Vienna. She still showed some traces of her former beauty and more than her share of insignificance. Her daughter-in-law, who brought one child after another into the world, handed them over to her, one after another, and then turned her attention to producing new children. Three died, although, in view of the progress of modern medicine, this was no longer customary.

In his last years, Alexander's grandfather Fries, the uninteresting businessman, had tried to make himself more important in the eyes of his grandson by confiding to him that the Fries family was probably related to the famous eighteenth-century bankers of the same name who had been made counts. But although old Fries, in his curiously belated urge to assert himself, brought up the subject again and again, Alexander Jessiersky never listened; nor did he think of the story after old Fries had died.

He lived entirely in a world of his own, though what kind of a world it was, no one—probably not even he himself—really knew. By day, he bestowed a modicum of attention upon the transport business, whose president he had become though his mother had inherited most of the company's stock. By night, he produced one child after another, less out of conviction than out of absentmindedness and because his wife set such great store by it. It must be said, however, that she remained pretty for a long time and did not make it difficult for him.

Chapter 3

Alexander Jessiersky, as we have said, did not devote very much time to his business. The company followed more or less of itself the course old Fries had laid down for it; transport business was about the only field in which that self-styled relative of the late Counts Fries had been competent.

But with the German occupation business suddenly boomed. To his credit, be it said that Alexander Jessiersky, little though he knew about business, did not particularly like this boom. For while he had little connection with his "shop," he was also sufficiently detached from it to mistrust the sudden spurt of activity. "Why," he asked himself, "should we go to the trouble of expanding when we can only do business that leads nowhere, since the profits cannot be used for our benefit, but are taken from us in taxes or must be reinvested in bad business? It is ridiculous to do a thing merely because others have become the slaves of the idea that one has to be 'active.' Are there not a thousand things to be attended to which, though much more important, are left undone? And does no one realize that all this frantic activity will result only in disaster—that disaster, in fact, has already overtaken us?"

But in the long run even this stubbornly inactive man could not escape the universal mania for activity. Early in 1940, his directors persuaded him that a certain property situated on the Southern Railroad had to be purchased in order to build new warehouses for the expanding concern. This property, however, belonged to a Count Luna. He had inherited it from his mother who, in a manner of speaking, had been a kind of Fries, that is, the stepdaughter of a manufacturer. Luna himself, however, had already gone one step beyond Alexander Jessiersky. Although he was not engaged in business, he did not want to sell the property because he had no confidence in the new currency introduced two years before.

"All right then," said Jessiersky to his directors. "That ends the matter. As you can see, he simply refuses to sell."

Then he would have to be made to hand it over, the directors told him. For what, after all, was one man's wish to hang onto idle real estate compared with the expansion needs of a big company?

With that he did not agree, returned Jessiersky. But, probably out of sheer laziness, he allowed his subordinates to do as they chose.

It was one of those periods when everything and anything could be taken away from a person, as long as it was declared to be to the advantage of the general public. And though the expropriation in the present case was rather to the advantage of a transport business which, to be sure, served the general public, the recalcitrant owner, Luna, was accused of belonging to certain monarchistic and, therefore, anti-German circles and put under arrest.

At this point Jessiersky awakened out of his indifference, but it was already too late. Luna was forced to hand over the property, and Jessiersky, although of course he no longer wanted to take the land, was forced to take it anyway. The maneuver should now have accomplished its purpose. But the Secret Police had become seriously interested in Luna's monarchism. They seized not only the proceeds from the forced sale, but all of his remaining possessions as well and sent him to the concentration camp at Mauthausen.

Jessiersky found the whole episode extremely painful. He told himself that, though he himself had not done anything, he had, out of his very inactivity, failed to do what should have been done. The few decent people still around began to avoid him. They did not, of course, dare to give him the cold shoulder for long, for they were afraid that he might make trouble for them through the connections that he so obviously possessed; they, therefore, soon sought him out once again. But Jessiersky was anything but relieved. That a misunderstanding could have such consequences, that the world was apparently ruled by misunderstandings, was profoundly distressing to him. All his efforts to get Luna out of Mauthausen proved unsuccessful, and it turned out that his supposed connections were not real connections after all. Luna remained in Mauthausen, and because Luna remained in Mauthausen, Jessiersky acquired the reputation of having really formidable connections. For at that time no one could believe that he might have used them, if he used them at all, not to keep a man in a concentration camp but to secure his release.

Faced with this miserable situation, in which his father, now reposing—as the son imagined—not in God, but in Poland, would have been quite in his element, Jessiersky was utterly bewildered and turned upon his directors who had got him into this affair. But he discovered that he did not even have the right to fire them. He then left no stone unturned in an effort to get them called up for army service; and in the case of two of them who, although overage, were reserve officers, he was successful. But his success gave him little cause for rejoicing, for both were delighted at the prospect of joining up or, at least, pretended they were. It was not until one of them was killed in France that Jessiersky experienced a measure of satisfaction; the more he thought about it, in fact, the more it pleased him. For this strange son of a colonel had a deep hatred of everything military, and death in action seemed to him the worst possible fate. He regarded it as the individual's ultimate betrayal by the community.

Finally he decided to call upon the relatives with whom Luna had formerly lived, with the intention of assuring them that he, Jessiersky, was not to blame for Luna's imprisonment. But he did not get very far. These persons, although related only to Luna's dead mother, were afraid their reputedly well-connected visitor might get them into trouble; relatives of a concentration camp inmate were frequently persecuted simply because they were related to him. The Millemoths, then—this was the name of the elderly couple—barely listened to Jessiersky's protestations that he could not be blamed for what had happened to Luna and cut short his derogatory remarks about the present regime and its cruelties. Supposing these remarks to have been made for the purpose of tricking them into betraying themselves, they hastened to assure him that Luna's reactionary tendencies had been well known, and they themselves disapproved of them highly. Far from being surprised at his arrest, they had considered it entirely justified. Surely a nation that had set out to conquer the world could not be expected to let a person who was blind to its greatness attack it from the rear. While they were not exactly happy that Luna had gone, for, after all, he was their relative, they had understood very well why he had been taken. In fact, they had been surprised that it had not happened long before. And so they went on, vying with each other in the anxious repetition of memorized phrases.

Jessiersky stared at them dumbfounded. At this moment, perhaps for the first time, there dawned upon this wealthy dreamer from the Strattmann Palace, who had had so little experience of hardship, some realization of the ugliness of life. He looked about the room and found it far more poorly furnished than he had expected. The Millemoths were by no means as well off as they had once been. They seemed, in fact, to have become quite impoverished; and while poverty in itself may not be degrading, it undoubtedly is when it follows immediately upon wealth. Luna himself, an unmarried man, appeared to have been by no means as well-to-do as might have been concluded from his former status as a real-estate owner. This made it all the more strange that he had been so unwilling to sell the property.

Luna was the son of a civil servant and had studied sociology; in fact, he had been on the point of applying for a lecturer's position at the university. But nothing explained why he had clung so obstinately to that property. Under normal conditions his refusal to sell would have made sense: rather than accept unreliable money for his last assets, he had preferred to live in reduced circumstances. But of what use had the lands been to him when he had practically starved because of them, and what use were they to him now in that camp where, again because of them, he was perhaps being beaten to death?

On a desk in the room stood a framed photograph; beside it, in a glass, a bunch of wild flowers.

"Is that he?" asked Jessiersky.

It was, in fact, his desk and his picture, and that the Millemoths had placed flowers beside it did not quite fit in with their professed satisfaction at his arrest. They became extremely embarrassed and reached for the picture to take it away.

"Never mind!" said Jessiersky and bent over to look at the picture.

It showed a slender, rather frail man in the garb of a Maltese Knight. The head seemed a little too large in proportion to the frail body. The face was long and narrow, the forehead high, the chin also long and somewhat protruding. It rested on the collar as though for support, or as though it were bound up in a cloth sling to keep the mouth from falling open like the chin of someone who has just died. The prominent forehead and chin made the middle part of the face look as if it had been pushed in. The man had the air of an elderly aristocrat, which formed a curious contrast with his obvious youthfulness. To heighten this contrast still further, there were two curved lines running from the nostrils to the corners of the mouth. When Jessiersky bent over to examine the picture more closely, he discovered that they were not single, but double lines, each with a ridge, forming a roll of skin between them. The hair was probably dark, the skin white, almost yellowish, and although the portrait had been retouched, the complexion looked as if it were pockmarked. About the eyes, however, there was a serene, almost sleepy, but nonetheless charming smile.

A silence had come over the room, and Jessiersky, who had the impression that the Millemoths might think that he was gloating over his victim, quickly straightened.

"Is the name Luna Italian?" he asked.

"No, Spanish," was the reply.

"He looks it," said Jessiersky. "And was he also a Chevalier de la Lune?"

The Millemoths did not understand this allusion.

"I mean was he—I should say, is he a Knight of Malta?"

"Yes."

Jessiersky had never met Luna, and as far as he could recall, he had never heard him mentioned by any of his acquaintances. Probably Luna's means did not permit him to go out very much. He had undoubtedly moved only in circles which, particularly now, for a variety of reasons, including financial, were closed to other people. He seemed, in any event, to belong to one of those foreign aristocratic families who appear in a country and remain for only a few decades. They attract little notice, neither have money nor know how to make it, and soon vanish from sight again. A sad existence, thought Jessiersky who, like all idle people, was fairly sociable.

"Is his father still living?" he asked.

"No."

"What was he?"

"Who?"

"The father."

"An official in the Ministry of Education."

"And has he any brothers and sisters?"

"The father?"

"The son."

"No—that is to say, yes. He had a brother who died before he himself came into the world."

Jessiersky again stooped down to examine the smile about Luna's eyes. When this was taken, he thought, the man probably did not even know why he was in such a good humor.

"And he is a sociologist, then?" he asked. "I mean …"

"Yes."

"What is a sociologist actually? I have a vague idea, but …"

"A sociologist," said Herr Millemoth, "is a kind of economist."

"That's what I thought," said Jessiersky. "By the way, do you believe it possible to restore order in the present chaos?"

He received no reply.

"From what I have heard," he said, "he was even planning to give lectures at the university."

"Yes."

"Did he run into any difficulties when he tried?"

"Oh, yes. He had a pronounced Catholic, that is to say, clerical bias ... which, combined with his other views, resulted in ..."

Jessiersky, feeling once again that the Millemoths thought they were being cross-examined, cut short this speech which would only have led to further groveling.

"Would to God," he exclaimed, "that the economy were still as he imagined it, for then neither the purchase nor the sale of his wretched piece of land would ever have been contemplated. But what really surprises me is that he seems to have had so little interest in putting his theories into practice." Here he looked about the room. "Could I perhaps do something to relieve his present situation? I mean, couldn't I place a certain sum at your disposal which would make it possible for you to send him food and clothing? I hear, to my horror, that the state seized not only the proceeds from the sale, but all the rest of his money as well, and perhaps you yourselves are not in a position to make any very great expenditure on his behalf...."

But he was hastily assured that in Mauthausen, Luna, like all the rest of the prisoners, wore a convict suit, that it was permitted to send him food only rarely, and that their means were sufficient for this. Jessiersky again received the impression that they thought he was trying to get them into trouble, that he might be drawing them out in order to discover whether they were sending illicit parcels to the prisoner. There was apparently nothing to be done with these people who were so terrified that they had become inordinately distrustful. So he shrugged his shoulders, took a last look at the photograph of the smiling Luna who had now even less to laugh about than before, and took leave of them. He found it particularly distressing when they put their farewell in the form of an awkward "Heil Hitler."

He left on foot, not having come by car because he did not

want his chauffeur to know where he had been. The dome of pale blue sky above the city reminded him for some reason of the sky over a steppe. The people in the street looked provincial, even shabby; fragments of conversation in a sloppy dialect reached his ears. He met no one he knew. He had time, therefore, both on his way back and after he reached the Strattmann Palace, amid its paintings, chandeliers, and tapestries, to think over this visit, Luna's ill-furnished apartment, and his plight in general. A great anger welled up in him against the wretched cautiousness and apprehensiveness of the Millemoths which had made it impossible for him to explain himself to them. These were no longer human beings, so he concluded, and it made no difference whether they were no longer so through their own fault or as a result of circumstances. Probably even Luna himself, in Mauthausen, was now no longer a human being! And it seemed to Jessiersky that he had brought misfortune not upon a human creature but upon an animal that had been full of trust in human beings: by a sudden movement, he, Jessiersky, had wounded it mortally—a dumb, unsuspecting animal.

He got up from the armchair in which he had been sitting and walked through the two big parlors and the dining room into the library, whose windows faced the courtyard. Out there it was as still as in the country. The light of the midday sun on the opposite wall was reflected into the two narrow rooms that made up the library. The gilt of the shelves on which the books were standing and the gold of the bindings gleamed as the light fell upon them. A clock was ticking.

Whenever Alexander Jessiersky entered this library, he was reminded of old Fries. He had to laugh when he thought of how utterly baffled his grandfather must have been by all these books. But in order to own such books and such a palace, it was no longer sufficient—as it had been in the case of the long extinct Strattmann family—to possess a large number of estates and to hold several well-paid court and army positions. Today it was necessary to be the owner of a transport business, of hideous warehouses, countless trucks and furniture vans, which were constantly moving back and forth between Brussels and Bucharest, between Copenhagen and Rome. The laborers and packers slaved away and shouted at one another; the trains roared and the locomotives whistled; even at night there was no quiet in the freight stations. But here in the library it was as still as in a cloister, and the ticking of the clock divided up eternity.

Alexander Jessiersky reached for the *Almanach de Gotha*. But he did not find the Lunas. He had almost begun to think that they were not real counts, but merely *conti*, and was just about to leave the library when, to make quite sure, he took out a Court Almanac and glanced through the table of contents. There, at last, he read: "… Löwenstein-Wertheim-Rochefort or Rosenberg, Lübeck, Lubomirski-Przevorsk, Lubomirski-Rzezov, Luchesi-Palli: see Campofranco, Lucedio, Lucinge; *Luna* see Villahermosa."

Under the heading "Villahermosa," however, he read: "Belonging to the house of Azlor de Aragon —Catholic.—Ancient Spanish nobility which appears as early as 1136 and whose line goes back to Blasco Perez de Azlor, born 1271, died 1286.—Noblemen (*ricos hombres*) of the old kingdom of Aragon; Baron Panzano 1293, Conde de Guara 1678." So they are merely *condes*, after all, thought Alexander Jessiersky. But it was to prove otherwise. "Inheritance of the dukedom of Villahermosa (Alfonso, a natural son of Juan 11, King of Aragon, Navarre, and Sicily, was named Duque de Villahermosa in 1476) and the earldom and dukedom of Luna (Juan de Aragon had been named Duque de Luna by his uncle, Ferdinand the Catholic, in 1512, and Conde de Luna by Philip III in 1604) following the marriage, in 1701, of Juan-Artel de Azlor, 2nd Conde de Guara, with Josefa de Gurrea de Aragon, Condesa de Luna...."

Who, among all these people, belonged to whom, and who was really descended from whom? Of one thing he was sure, however: the name of the prisoner in Mauthausen was not both Villahermosa and Luna, but simply Luna. The holders of these titles of count and duke had continually changed. It might very well be, therefore, that the forebears of this unfortunate man had possessed the title of count only temporarily, but had continued to use it anyway. Occasionally, however, the earldom had even become a dukedom. In wartime, for instance, the Count of Luna had also had command of the contingents from the neighboring counties. But it seemed most unlikely that the man in Mauthausen was a Spanish duke and, to top that, related to the Kings of Aragon.

Further down in the section on the Villahermosas, the reader was referred to Bethencourt, *Historia genealogica y heraldica de la monarquia española.* So without losing himself further in the maze of titles of the still living Villahermosas, Duques de Granada de Ega, Condes de Guara, Vizcondes de Muruzabal de Andion y de Zolina, etc., Alexander Jessiersky went in search of the Bethencourt. But he could not find the book. Where it was, Heaven only knew. It had been there, it was listed in the catalogue, but it had been taken out. Even the Strattmann library, despite the shipping business by which it was maintained, was crumbling away. Probably in the end it, like so many other things, would also completely disintegrate. Such establishments really lived only on borrowed time, for all that the library clock pretended that the time there was eternal. It was not. It was time exactly like any other. For when the clock, by its ticking, sliced off single segments of it, what was left was no longer as large as true eternity. By reason of this very ticking, slicing off, hacking off, "eternity"

31

became smaller, gradually shrank, and would ultimately come to an end. This was the proof that there was no real eternity, no really enduring time in the library.

Jessiersky finally abandoned his search for the Bethencourt. In various other works, however, he found that there had originally been a Don Alvaro de Luna, whose ancestry could not be readily traced, but who seemed to have been of very high birth. He may even, like the rest of the Spanish high nobility, have traced his ancestry to the Visigoth kings; just as the most noble houses of Europe, the Hapsburgs, for example, the Lorraine dynasty, or the Guelfs, claimed descent from a legendary Frankish King Faramund who, in turn, so the story ran, was descended from the Queen of Troy. No one, of course, could follow them as far back as all that. But although Don Alvaro's ancestors were shrouded in misty twilight, his descendants, or one of them at least, stood out in bold relief. His natural son, Alvaro, later raised to the rank of Count Gormas, had been Constable of Castile. In 1453 he was executed because, having married the Infanta Maria of Portugal, he had presumed to put himself forward as the brother-in-law of the King. It seemed quite likely that the unfortunate Luna might have been a descendant of this Bastard. Later on, neither the Vil lahermosas nor the Lunas themselves, but quite another family, the Moncadas, had possessed Luna.

Jessiersky discovered also that in the city of Leon there was still a Luna Palace. Luna itself, an old capital city of the Lusitanians (which also suggested some connection with nearby Luesia), was situated south of the Pyrenees between the two arms of the river Arva, not far from Exea de los Caballeros and Saragossa. Long ago the city must have been important, for the country below Luna was still called Cataluna, the "Land below Luna," Catalonia. But now the city had most probably become a dreadful hole.

There was also a French family, de Viel de Lunas d'Espeuilles. But these Lunas lived in southern France. In eastern France there was Lunéville, in Brussels a rue de la Lune, in Italy a Portus Lunae, so named by the Romans because of its half-moon shape, and the village of Lunigiana in the former duchy of Massa-Carrara. In the northern part of Lower Austria, there was the so-called Moon Forest, in Upper Austria the Moon Lake, and in Africa there were the Mountains of the Moon from which the Nile rises. And finally there was Monday and the moon itself. But that Luna had originally come from the moon was improbable, although his face was shaped like a half moon and had a moonlike smile.

Alexander Jessiersky spent many hours in the library, and when he left it, it was far into the evening. On the table in the middle of the front room lay a pile of books, and the ticking of the clock went on and on dividing up eternity, which was not eternity, and converting it into time.

Jessiersky's visit to the Millemoths had taken place in September, 1940. During the years that followed, he inquired repeatedly after Luna by roundabout ways. He also gave him assistance whenever possible by sending him food parcels and such like.

Whether or not Luna knew that all or most of the food parcels which he received came from Jessiersky, it is impossible to say. Perhaps he knew and simply pretended that he did not know, or perhaps he merely accepted them. A concentration camp was not the place to make a show of manly pride when it came to food parcels. In any case, with the aid of the parcels, he bore up under the hardships of his place of detention and the rigors of forced labor, in spite of, or perhaps because of, his frailty and flexibility, far better than more robust people, many of whom did not survive them at all. These hardships and rigors, as everyone knows (although the entire nation later disclaimed all knowledge of them), were appalling. It was understandable, of course, that the Third Reich, like so many other empires before it, should keep slaves. What was not understandable was that, unlike other slaveholding regimes, it treated its slaves so miserably that it destroyed their capacity for work and, along with it, their usefulness, or potential usefulness. What is more, in so doing, it merely damaged still further its already bad reputation and made more and more enemies. Both government and people succeeded only in injuring themselves when they allowed the jailers to give full rein to their cruelty. The jailers alone derived a dubious pleasure from this license. And it is more than strange that the Third Reich, which permitted no one any pleasure, should have allowed them this satisfaction.

In June, 1944, Jessiersky learned that Luna had been transferred to the camp at Ebensee. There, salt was mined in a manner which was extremely uncomfortable for those who were mining it, and the casualties among the forced laborers were high. But why should salt be mined in a more comfortable way when everything else in the hard-pressed Reich had become as uncomfortable as possible?

Jessiersky decided to leave Vienna and its growing discomforts. Relying on his directors to see that the freight cars of the company, which were being hit more and more frequently by dive-bombers, were kept rolling within the steadily shrinking sphere of German world domination, he slipped off to Zinkeneck with his family. In Zinkeneck, he used enough of the tactical talent inherited from his father to keep from having to bear arms. He took up arms only to the extent of walking in the valley with a hunting rifle slung over his shoulder, scanning the high ravines through his field glasses for chamois, whose complete indifference to historical events he thus tried to emulate. In January,

1945, he buried his mother who died as insignificantly as she had lived. In March, he got his wife pregnant with yet another child, although this time he began to feel slightly overwhelmed by all this childbearing.

Meanwhile, the armies on all fronts had been practically routed, so that at the end of April, and the beginning of May there was a veritable invasion of Zinkeneck by generals, members of the general staff, and officers of the quartermasters' corps. These were the remnants of no less than four army divisions, and when there was no longer an army of any sort, they came pouring into the few valleys the world empire had been reduced to. In comradely fashion, each of the generals tried to get the so-called castle entirely for himself. They argued so long over this weighty matter that in the end no one moved in, and all of them had to pull off their riding boots in mad haste and put on requisitioned hobnail shoes to flee into the mountains. They were soon brought back, however, to take up quarters behind barbed wire. Alexander Jessiersky bitterly regretted that his father who, had he still been alive, would undoubtedly have been advanced to the rank of general, was not among them.

Immediately after the collapse, Jessiersky began to make inquiries as to whether Luna had come out alive. But although he expended a great deal of time and effort, he was unable to get any information. It was impossible to discover anything about him. He was definitely not among the living, but neither was he among the dead, at least according to the records. Jessiersky then wrote from Zinkeneck to all the military hospitals in the vicinity of Ebensee to ask whether Luna might have been brought into one of them. But he was not to be found among all the living skeletons that had been admitted. It could only be concluded, therefore, that, in the general confusion of the last weeks of war, he had died of hunger or had been murdered and that his body had been burned, or buried in some unknown place.

Jessiersky did hear, however, that the Millemoths had recovered from their fright (which was no slight matter, since in the end they had been even more terrified of their liberators than of their oppressors) and had denounced him for having Luna on his conscience. But since Zinkeneck was in the American Zone, their denunciations were of no avail. By the time the charge was brought in, the American troops had long since turned their entire attention to the female domestic servants in the zone and other ladies of this sort. Even the American commanders were already beginning to turn their attention from the political quarrels within the country to their own extrapolitical conflicts.

They were, of course, quite ignorant of Continental conditions. But with the complete assurance of sleepwalkers, they fished out the so-called Fascist elements of the population which they had just been fighting, and cast suspicion on the so-called non-Fascist. Supported in their activities, commercial and otherwise, by the so-called Fascists, without whom, in fact, they would have been unable to carry out this policy, they began to build up a barricade against their former so-called ally in the east. Viewed from the standpoint of this policy of theirs, the war against the Third Reich had been only a minor conflict whose importance had been greatly exaggerated. Even the death of the thirty-five million people, which the Third Reich had on its conscience, had been an episode of greatly overestimated significance. In other words, the loss of those multitudes had been no more than an episode which it was perfectly all right to forget and which, in fact, was forgotten in no time at all. For actually figures mean nothing or almost nothing. When, for example, there were only two men in the world, Cain and Abel (for Adam did not really count any more), Abel's death should have mattered much more than now the loss of one and one-half percent of the world's population. But it turned out that Abel's death did not matter a bit. For Cain propagated, and the present population of the earth will propagate with or without that one and one-half percent....

Although Alexander Jessiersky had not been a Fascist or anything resembling a Fascist—nor, to be sure, the opposite of one—he remained in Zinkeneck, to be on the safe side, for two more years, for he had no desire to fall victim to any political stupidities. Finally, however, he returned to Vienna. There, very much against his will, he was forced to attend to so many things that he forgot Luna who, until then, had still occupied his thoughts from time to time. Had Luna reappeared he would undoubtedly have repaid Jessiersky for all that had been done to him—even without American help, even against the opposition of his own now so conciliatory Rightist circles. Luna, however, was still among the missing.

But about 1949 certain things occurred that led Jessiersky to conclude that Luna was still alive.

the remains
watch imagining
an eye on
him
nk of had
the planks there
joined to them. But
longer existed.
it that had also

Chapter 4

At this time Jessiersky was still busy with the restoration of the Strattmann Palace which, having come through the bombing without being completely demolished, had been what was described as "moderately plundered" during the liberation of the city.

Practically everyone had had a hand in the looting, not only the military but also the civilian population. Reportedly even certain people belonging to the best circles, or what still passed for such, had availed themselves of this opportunity to make provision for the hard days of peace ahead.

In order to replace a painting which had fallen prey either to an infantryman of artistic tastes, or to the foraging of a certain high-placed civil servant who shortly thereafter had betaken himself to Linz, Alexander Jessiersky had started negotiations for the purchase of a large portrait. Its subject was an unknown periwigged gentleman wearing a cuirass and a silk sash, and displaying the Cross of the Teutonic Order. This was not the first likeness of a stranger that Jessiersky had purchased; but he always felt rather foolish when he bought one; for months afterward, it seemed to look disparagingly down at him from the wall.

One afternoon, in an effort to discover the identity of the man in the cuirass and wig—whom, without the flicker of an eyelash, his father would have passed off as an ancestor—Jessiersky was leafing through certain volumes in the Strattmann library which contained engravings of generals and other celebrities, together with ample explanatory notes. His children had gathered about him and were looking over his shoulder. One of them, a girl, the one who had been conceived in the late winter of 1945 and who by now was no longer the youngest, but the next youngest, suddenly pointed her finger at one of the pictures and exclaimed: "That's he!"

"Who?" asked Jessiersky and looked more closely at the engraving. It was not the man with the periwig and the Cross of the Teutonic Order, but it resembled someone else, someone who seemed vaguely familiar. For a moment he could not remember who it was. Then suddenly he knew. It reminded him of Luna. "Who?" repeated Jessiersky. "Who is that? What do you mean? How could you know him, you silly child!"

"But that's the man we saw out walking!" said the girl.

"Out walking where?"

"In the Volksgarten."

Jessiersky stared at the child and then back again at the page. The man in the engraving was actually a Dutchman, General Knobelsdorff de Nijenhuis, but he reminded him very much of Luna.

"What do you mean in the Volksgarten?" cried Jessiersky.

According to the little girl, the children, who regularly took a walk in that public park with their French governess, had been spoken to several times by a man who resembled the man in the picture. The other children also confirmed this. Only he was dressed differently. He had given sweets to the children, or rather to the next youngest, whom he called his little friend—always to the next youngest, although the others had also begged him for some.

To the children's astonishment, their father became extremely excited. "Mademoiselle!" he shouted. "Have Mademoiselle come at once!"

At the sound of his angry voice, Mademoiselle came running and so did Elisabeth Jessiersky.

"How could you allow the children to be fed by a perfectly strange man, not once, but several times?" he asked the governess, his agitation increasing. "Who knows what kind of filthy stuff he may have given them to eat! What did he look like? Like the man in this picture?" And he thrust General Knobelsdorff under her nose.

"Please!" exclaimed Elisabeth Jessiersky, who was utterly bewildered by all this, for he did not ordinarily take such an interest in the children's affairs. "Don't get so excited! Whatever *is* the matter?"

"Be quiet!" cried Jessiersky, and Mademoiselle, who was looking at the picture, stammered that yes, he might have looked something like that, the dispenser of the sweetmeats, a charming man and very kind to the children, particularly to the next youngest whom he called his little ...

"Do you know what you are?" Jessiersky interrupted her. "You are a stupid cow!" But he shouted this in French, and as in French "vaches" is also a name for the police, Mademoiselle took it that she was supposed to have called the police.

No, she hadn't called the police, she faltered, there had been no necessity for that....

Really, it would have been better for Alexander Jessiersky if he had learned some colloquial French from his late father who had been so good at it. "Tomorrow," he shouted, "you'll go to the Volksgarten with the children and I'll follow behind and look at the fellow myself!"

"But certainly!" stammered Mademoiselle, "certainly, sir!"

Elisabeth Jessiersky shook her head. "You simply can't afford to get so wrought up over every little thing!" she exclaimed.

Jessiersky did not reply. During dinner he spoke scarcely a word and simply stared into space. Later that evening, he made no move to lay the foundation for a new child, nor did he do so on any of the following evenings.

For when he went the next day to the Volksgarten, walking quite inconspicuously behind the children, the man who looked like General Knobelsdorff did not appear. Nor was there any sign of him on the days following, although Jessiersky slipped in with the utmost caution, a great distance behind the little group. Then it rained for a few days, and afterward the children kept having to go again and again to the Volksgarten until they became bored and begged to be allowed to go to the Stadtpark. But the man who was the image of General Knobelsdorff did not show himself again, and his obstinate failure to appear so obsessed Jessiersky that he could think of nothing else, and all consideration for his wife's amorous desires passed from his mind completely.

Then the whole family went off to Zinkeneck and stayed there until autumn and all that time Jessiersky thought about Knobelsdorff. Only after they had returned to Vienna did he come to believe that the materialization of Knobelsdorff had been pure coincidence, and he began to forget him. He was just on the point of turning his attention once more to his wife when something occurred which, in a most painful way, brought back the memory of Knobelsdorff and with it that of Luna.

The next youngest fell ill and, although a great deal of time had elapsed since her encounter with the man in the park, Jessiersky leaped to the conclusion that the illness was a result of the sweets. All along he had been secretly afraid of something like that!

This man who was the image of Knobelsdorff, he decided, must have been Luna, after all. But he was not sure whether he should worry most about the child, about the other children—who might also fall ill, each in turn—about his wife, or about himself. What he could not understand was why Luna had given the candy only to the next youngest and not to the other children as well.

Perhaps the man had conceived the diabolical plan of killing the children not all at once, but one by one. It would be like Luna to do something like that. He had not simply appeared and said: "Here I am and I demand the punishment of all those who are to blame for my misfortune." From the outset, and probably quite justifiably, he had not relied on any of the authorities to track down the guilty people. Instead, after hiding out for a long time, God knew where and why, he had taken it into his own hands to mete out the punishment! From out of the darkness into which he had been forced and in which he may have decided to continue to dwell, from out of the realm of the living dead he had been banished to, from out of an invisible, incomprehensible region, he began to take revenge! And to make it as frightful as possible, he had waited for months, for years, himself inaccessible, inexorable; now he would strike not only the guilty, but also the innocent, and thereby once again the guilty, the one guilty man, exacting vengeance doubly, triply, a hundredfold....

But when Jessiersky reached this point in his thinking, or rather when his terrified imaginings had brought him to these confused conclusions, he told himself that it was too soon to give way to panic. Luna, after all, had not only to plan, but also to carry out that horrible scheme. His first attempt had met with a crucial setback when Jessiersky had discovered that he still existed! By sheer chance he had discovered it, but he had discovered it nonetheless. The fact of his survival had been revealed, and now if Luna chose to make trouble, the trouble could be traced to its source, and it would be possible to put a stop to his activities—which, otherwise, would not have been the case.

"I shall simply have to tell the bastard what a mistake he is making," muttered Jessiersky to himself. "I must find the opportunity to make it clear to him that I am not to blame for his misfortune. I must force him to meet me! As far as I am concerned, he can pay back those scoundrels of directors and he can mete out punishment to *them*. But he is not going to persecute me and my family. And he shall have back his damned property, tax free, cost free, at once!"

With these thoughts milling about in his mind, he hurried over to call on the Millemoths. For who but the Millemoths should know where Luna might be found?

The feelings of the Millemoths had undergone yet another transformation in that they had long since regretted having denounced Jessiersky as the author of Luna's misfortune. From the fact that the denunciation had produced no result whatsoever, they had concluded—and probably correctly—that the political weathercock, having swung around once, had now veered back again, and was pointing in the same direction as before. And when they saw Jessiersky appearing, they experienced the same terror that had assailed them when he had called on them the first time.

This time Frau Millemoth did not merely make an attempt, as she had ten years earlier, to put Luna's picture away. While her husband talked to the visitor in the foyer, she actually managed to get it out of the way. The picture, however, was no longer in Luna's room, which had been sublet. It was in the Millemoths' own room.

"We are not quite so well off as we were when you gave us the pleasure of your first visit, Herr Jessiersky," said Millemoth with as much amiability as he could muster. "This time we shall have to receive you in our bedroom. My wife is just putting it in order. We had to rent the room of our unfortunate ... that is, of our poor … I mean, of our cousin … where we received you before. The situation, alas, and not only economically, has very much changed since we had the honor of making your acquaintance. It has, in fact, become quite intolerable."

"You think so?" said Jessiersky, wondering how he could get any information about Luna's whereabouts out of this coward.

"I should say so!" exclaimed Millemoth. "Utterly intolerable! It's true right down the line, from the biggest things to the smallest. You have no idea what difficulties we have had, for example, with this business of renting the room."

"You had?" inquired Jessiersky. "What kind of difficulties?"

"Troubles with our tenant."

"You've had trouble with him?"

"Nothing but trouble, Herr Jessiersky."

"In what way?"

"He won't move out."

"Why?"

"Because he maintains that he has lived in it now for more than a half year, and nowadays it is illegal to put anyone out of a room that he has occupied for over six months. You can't for the life of you get rid of a fellow like that."

"Do you want to rent it to someone else, then?"

"Of course. That, too. We have had several much better offers. But the main thing is that this particular person gets on our nerves."

"I can quite understand," said Jessiersky, "if he is one of those persons who refuse to leave…. Who is he anyway?"

"The tenant?"

"Yes."

"A man by the name of Berdiczewer."

"A Pole?"

"More or less. But he apparently did not like it in his own country, and so he came to Vienna. He can go wherever he wants, for all I care. But to our misfortune he came to us, and now we can't get him out."

"And what if your cousin should come back?" Jessiersky inquired suddenly, carefully studying Millemoth's face.

"I beg your pardon?"

"If Count Luna were to come back—wouldn't you be able to get Herr Berdiczewer out then?"

"Then, perhaps," said Millemoth. "But he, alas, will never come back, our poor ... that is our ..."

Jessiersky watched him closely for a moment or two, then he said: "But how does it happen that a person with a name like your tenant's managed to get through the entire war without ... Things were bad enough here, but in Poland they must have been absolutely ..."

"He wasn't in Poland then."

"He wasn't?"

"No."

"But in—?"

"I beg your pardon?"

"Where was he during the war?"

"In Portugal."

"In Portugal? Why didn't he stay there?"

"How do I know? At any rate he went back to Poland at the end of the war. But apparently he couldn't stick it out there either, and so he came to Vienna."

"Well, well," said Jessiersky, "there are all kinds of Poles, some agreeable, some not so agreeable.... But let's change the subject! Don't you think that this conversation right outside the door of Herr Berdiczewer is ..."

"We couldn't care less," said Millemoth. "Let him hear it! I certainly don't feel obliged to show him any consideration."

"Very well," said Jessiersky, "but I think that …"

Millemoth, however, interrupted him with unaccustomed vehemence. "But if times were what they were once," he shouted in so loud a voice that Herr Berdiczewer could not help but hear it in his room, "he certainly wouldn't be here any longer. He would be elsewhere, believe me!"

"That's possible," said Jessiersky, "quite, quite possible. For when times were different, your own cousin did not go on living in that room. He, too, was elsewhere. Or have you forgotten that?"

But Millemoth had no chance to reply. For at this moment Frau Millemoth appeared and invited the men to come into the other room.

"I have come to see you," said Jessiersky, when he had seated himself in the Millemoths' bedroom, "to ask you—and I want you to tell me quite frankly—whether you happen to know where your cousin, Count Luna, is at present."

The Millemoths stared at him in astonishment, or at least they assumed an expression of astonishment.

"What I mean to say," went on Jessiersky, "is that I know that he is in Vienna. What I would like to learn from you, therefore, is simply where he is living. Where can I find him?" To give the impression of calm superiority, he took out his cigarettes, put one in his mouth, lighted it, and crossed his legs.

There was another silence. Finally Millemoth said: "You want to find him? Speak to him? I scarcely believe, Herr Jessiersky, that your desire is strong enough to induce you to commit suicide on the chance of finding the poor fellow."

Jessiersky interrupted him with a wave of his cigarette. "I know that he is alive," he said. "I have already told you that."

The Millemoths again looked at each other as though to confirm their opinion that this visitor, who had already delivered Luna to the executioner and had tried to do the same to them, was again threatening to bring disaster upon them, probably because of their denunciation.

"Herr Jessiersky," said Frau Millemoth, "if our poor cousin were still alive, he would certainly have come to see us."

"That, unfortunately, is not so certain," said Jessiersky. "For if I were your cousin, for example, and had the intentions that he has, or appears to have, I probably would not have called on you, either. You two, to be quite frank, seem, to me, at least, not reliable enough—don't misunderstand me—too easily influenced and not courageous enough for someone who would want you to keep your mouths shut, to let no one squeeze anything out of you—to repose any special confidence in you. Still, Luna may have been indiscreet enough to let you know that he's still alive. And because he *might* have committed this indiscretion, I am here and I now ask you: where is he? To be frank again, I'll tell you that I am determined to make use of every means at my disposal to get this information out of you. For it is extremely important to me." And with these words, as though to emphasize his determination, he ground out his cigarette.

"But we don't know! We honestly don't know!" cried Millemoth, his self-possession dwindling. "Why in the world are you, who should know better than anyone else that he is dead, suddenly telling us that he's still alive?"

Jessiersky looked out of the window without replying. The Millemoths' apartment was high up. A late autumn storm had swept swirls of yellow smoke from a chimney down over the dirty tile roofs; and the wooded hills, which could usually be seen in the distance, were concealed behind a curtain of rain. "Say nothing for a moment," thought Jessiersky, "just say nothing, so that these people will lose their nerve! For if they don't lose it, they will never tell me where he is."

"Tell us!" Millemoth suddenly said. "If it's so important to you as you say, you will admit that it is important for us also to find out whether or not he is really alive!"

"How often," said Jessiersky, "do I have to repeat this to you? He *is* alive."

"But how do you know?"

Jessiersky shrugged his shoulders. "I just know," he said.

"The last news we had from him," said Frau Millemoth, "was in March four years ago. He did write us then that things were going well with him...."

"Which, after all, means nothing," said Jessiersky. "What else would he have written from *there?* That things were going badly?"

"Precisely," said Frau Millemoth.

"I hope at least," said Jessiersky, "that the parcels I sent him proved useful—I mean that they were actually delivered to him."

"We, too, sent parcels," said Frau Millemoth. "But from April 1945 until today we have had not a single word from him."

"Because he was killed!" Millemoth exclaimed. "Because he is dead! As long as he was in the camp, he was well taken care of, not only thanks to our gifts and yours, but by the camp itself. But the moment our so-called liberators arrived, the organization broke down completely and the prisoners were left to starve!"

"That's going too far!" cried Jessiersky. "Or do you really mean to tell me that you think it was the so-called liberators and not the Germans who were responsible for the huge piles of starved corpses which were afterward pictured everywhere! Unfortunately, those photographs are no longer being published. But it might bring people like you to their senses, Herr Millemoth, if the newspapers would continue to drive those atrocities home to us at least once a week!"

"I was only trying to say," protested Millemoth, "that the Allied invasion made it impossible for the Germans to take proper care of the camp."

"Oh come!" Jessiersky said. "Surely you are only pretending to be a Fascist because you think I am one myself and because you think the Fascists are about to come back into power now! Let's have no more of these stupidities, Herr Millemoth! Though you are no hero, you are a decent person, and I, too, I hope, am a decent person. What is more, I am far too incompetent, or at any rate too apathetic, a businessman to want to advance my company by improper means. To be quite precise, I don't care a fig for the company. I never cared about it. It was not I but my directors who sent your cousin to the prison camp. But they were able to do this because I paid so little attention to what was going on. This I freely admit and realize that I am, therefore, to blame, too, in a way. But I regret my indolence which proved so disastrous for your cousin. God knows I regret it! So tell me where the unfortunate man is, for it would be senseless to keep it from me. You can feel free to tell me!"

The Millemoths looked at him for a moment doubtfully. Finally Herr Millemoth said: "I swear to you I don't know. What is more, I really don't believe you when you say that he is still alive."

"But he is," said Jessiersky. "He definitely is alive."

"Then what proof have you?"

"The following," said Jessiersky who, meanwhile, had made up his mind to lay his cards on the table. And he told the Millemoths what had happened to the next youngest.

When he had finished, there was a pause. "I simply can't believe that of our cousin!" exclaimed Millemoth.

"I could," said Jessiersky. "For if what happened to him had happened to me, I would probably do just what he's doing. Only first, *I* would have got more accurate information as to who was to blame for my misfortune and who was not. To make this quite clear—that's why I am so anxious to talk to him."

"And the little girl?" asked Frau Millemoth. "What disease did she have? What do the doctors say?"

Jessiersky shrugged his shoulders. "At first the doctors thought it might be diabetes," he replied. "But she had none of the characteristic symptoms. So they began to look for sources of infection that might have been connected with the growth of her second teeth. But they found none. Now they think it is simply a sepsis."

"But for goodness' sake," Millemoth cried out, "you don't get a sepsis from candy."

"Not as a rule," Jessiersky said. "But it's possible. Let us assume, for example, that those candies contained a poison which did not penetrate the entire body, but attacked the walls of the stomach and intestines. Then a sepsis might quite easily develop."

"We swear to you by all that is sacred to us," said Millemoth, "that for years we have neither seen nor heard from our poor cousin. You told us before that you regarded us as decent people, and it would, in fact, be senseless to pretend that we mourn the Third Reich. We are, if you really wish to know, monarchists, just as our poor cousin was, and we believe in all that is held sacred under a monarchy—in God, for example. We swear to you by God, therefore, that we do not know where Count Luna is, or even that he still *is*. Since we more than doubt that he is alive, we, alas, can't tell you anything about him."

"Show me his picture again," said Jessiersky after a moment.

Frau Millemoth took the picture out of the drawer in which she had hidden it.

Jessiersky examined it closely for a long time. "Yes, that is he," he said at last.

"Of course it is he," said Millemoth.

"I mean he looks exactly like General Knobelsdorff. And the man who fed my daughter candies also looks like General Knobelsdorff. So it follows that he also resembles Count Luna and since this kind of face, nowadays at least, is more than unusual, the man might very well have been Count Luna."

"But did you really see him? Did you talk with him?"

"No. Unfortunately, I am only getting to know him now."

"But you can't tell anything from pictures. And merely because your Mademoiselle, who is probably just as silly as most governesses, said that …"

"The children said so, too."

"Yes—but they are just children."

"But we have nothing to go on but the evidence of the children, the governess, and the pictures. Produce Luna for me. Then—perhaps—I will change my opinion. But since, as you say, you cannot …"

"Not even God Almighty could do that!"

Jessiersky again looked out of the window. Smoke was no longer pouring from the chimney, only a flickering film of hot air. Above the wooded hills pale sunbeams could be seen here and there darting through the cloud bank. But the storm was still raging about the house and there was a bad draft in the Millemoths' bedroom. Jessiersky got to his feet. He said: "It gives one a strange feeling not to be able to find out anything about a certain person, and even less to speak to him—whether because he will not allow himself to be spoken to or because he is really dead. But we spend our lives behind a wall. We ask again and again, and no one and nothing gives us any answer—not even God. He least of all …

Well, in any event, if ever you should really hear from Luna, let me know...."

"Of course."

"... for after all, even you would not be wholly indifferent if he were wandering about in this fashion."

"No, we would certainly not be indifferent. Only, as I said before, I do not believe ..."

But Jessiersky had already turned to Frau Millemoth and was kissing her hand. Then he left the room and Millemoth accompanied him to the foyer which smelled of kerosene.

In the hallway, Jessiersky paused once more. "But if you should happen to see your cousin," he said, "you can tell him this for me. If he continues to avoid me, if, as he has, he persists in hiding in the darkness, if he goes on doing what he is doing now, if he does not come and find me and say quite openly, 'Here I am,' I shall behave toward him as he is behaving toward me. Since he is taking every liberty, I shall do likewise, and I will regard him as a self-declared outlaw, as fair game which may be shot down wherever it is found. And tell him also that I know very well how this is done, because I own a hunting preserve where I can learn this sort of thing. And that I can get a great deal of practice because it is a vast place!" And with that he left Millemoth, who was struggling to find words with which to reply, and went out of the apartment.

So ended this visit which, while not accomplishing its purpose, had an unexpected consequence. Herr Berdiczewer, who had overheard the conversation outside his door—talk about changes in the political situation and even about shooting people down—ceased to feel at ease with the Millemoths. That very day he rented a room elsewhere, and on the following day he moved out.

Chapter 5

As the winter went on, the condition of the next youngest continued to improve. But whereas, in the fall, Jessiersky had been on the verge of forgetting all about the adversary who had not reappeared, the man now was never out of his thoughts. That the little girl was feeling better and none of the other children had fallen ill, he attributed solely to the fact that he had stood guard over his family all the time, "like the devil," to prevent Luna from doing any further harm.

Truth to tell, most of the time he merely sat in the library engrossed in finding out as much as he could about Luna's ancestry. He had the two rooms heated with a wood fire, and enveloped in the smell of burning logs, he would explore the subject of Luna and his forebears, giving free rein to his imagination rather than evaluating the facts. Since he felt that his own character could be explained best by that of the Jessierskys, it seemed to him that Luna's nature might be revealed to him through a study of the Luna family. He would then know what to expect and how to guard against his attacks. In any case he had no choice but to deal with his enemy in this speculative fashion, for all during this period Luna gave no sign of life.

In the course of these ruminations, Luna's ancestors began to merge with his own. And not only the ancestors, but also the times and the places and Luna and he himself, Jessiersky, all began to become confused in his mind. He could not help thinking, for example, that the Constable of Castile (from whom, as it had turned out, Luna was descended), that quixotic Bastard who had wanted to be recognized as the brother-in-law of John the Second, must have been very much like Pavel Alexandrovich Jezierskij who had been the brother-in-law of the rich Raczynskis. It seemed to him that the Luna Palace in Leon could not have looked very different from the Strattmann Palace in Vienna. He became convinced—and this he had admitted quite freely to the Millemoths—that if what had happened to his enemy had happened to him, he would have behaved no differently than this enemy of his.

Jessiersky did not, of course, find in his library all the books he needed for his investigations. He, therefore, went to the public libraries for what he lacked and also went over a large number of still unpublished documents in the State Archives. This was a considerable undertaking, for the Lunas, although of distinguished origin, had centuries earlier sunk into insignificance and oblivion, and any marks they might have made on history had gone with the wind. A study of the *Cronica de Alvaro de Luna*, Caribay's *Compendio historial de las ordenes militares*, the *Annales* of Zurita, and similar tomes, as well as the works of some Austrian historians and a considerable number of imperial edicts and special decrees, revealed the following facts:

Alvaro de Luna, Count of Gormas, Constable of Castile, and Grand Master of the Order of Santiago, favorite and minister of John the Second, after having paved the way for the marriage of his master to Isabella of Portugal, managed also to ally himself with the Lusitanian kings by espousing Isabella's sister, the Infanta Maria. At first the marriage was kept secret, but later on the practically omnipotent favorite decided to appear publicly as the brother-in-law of the ruler. Whereupon the House of Trastamara, which he had served for thirty years with such profit to himself that his estates had become bigger than those of all the rest of the Castilian nobility combined, withdrew its favor, and on the scaffold of Valladolid he met his end. Following the gruesome custom of the day, the executioner thrust his knife into his victim's neck and then, in a rather leisurely fashion, proceeded to sever the head from the body. Some months afterward, Maria of Portugal gave birth to the fruit of her alliance with the adventurer, a boy, also named Alvaro. Of all his father's vast estates, not an acre was left him, and throughout his life, he was hated by the royal house.

For centuries this branch of the Luna family virtually vanished from the scene. As beggarly hangers-on of the great, they passed their lives in utter poverty—a state which they shared with one million petty nobles and seven million still poorer peasants and laborers. It was not until 1700 that a certain Inigo de Luna emerged from this misery, and, in fact, it is not altogether certain that he was descended from the Constable. This man went to Vienna with one of the groups of Spanish nobles who were sent there at more or less regular intervals to serve at the imperial court. He distinguished himself in the wars against the Turks and was invested by Charles the Sixth with two estates in Hungary, Györkeny and Czecze.

When he reached this point in his reading, Jessiersky turned pale. For "Györkeny" and "Czecze" were the titles of one of his own grandmothers, that Sophie Grabaricz de Györkeny and Czecze, who had been the wife of Witold Jessiersky. In what order the Lunas and the Grabariczes had been invested with those estates and when they had lost them (for, like the Jessierskijs, the Lunas had also lost them) was of no importance compared to the fact that a link of this sort existed between the two families. In itself, it was not particularly significant since very often two entirely different families were invested one after the other with the same estate. But to Jessiersky it was of the utmost significance, for it confirmed him in his mysterious feeling of oneness with his mortal enemy.

At the time of Ferdinand the First, also called the Kind, a Luna served a term as ambassador to the Holy See and was also made a count in his own right, that is, independent of the Spanish earldom which long before had been transferred to the Villahermosas. Afterward, however, the family sank once again into obscurity. Luna's father, to be sure, had married a Baroness Judt-Hofkirchen, whose mother, after the death of her first husband, had married a manufacturer name Millemoth. But the Millemoths had, meanwhile, become just as impoverished as the Lunas. Virtually the last remnant of the Millemoth fortune had been the property on the Southern Railroad—whose purchase by the Fries concern had not only proved disastrous for Luna himself, but also began the undoing of Alexander Jessiersky.

On the night when his research on this sad, strange subject came to an end, Jessiersky thoughtfully shoved into a heap the books, letters, and photostats which were lying about on the library table. Then he took down from one of the shelves Coello's *Atlas de España* and opened to the region of the Pyrenees in order to look for the city of Luna. After a few moments he found the little, now apparently quite unimportant, town from which Luna had come and, with him, all these woes. Actually there was not much to see on the small map. But in spite, or perhaps because, of this, it suddenly seemed to Jessiersky that the landscape on the map bore a certain resemblance to the landscape of the moon. It is possible, even probable, that this was the moment at which, first only in a very vague way, but later more and more definitely, he began to identify Luna with the moon, or at least to identify the influence which Luna exercised with that exercised by the moon.

He knew by now that the name Luna did not derive from the satellite of the earth, but came from the Alani, a tribe that some time in the fourth century A.D. had left their original home in the Wolkonski forest in Russia, had reached Spain on their migration, and, before moving on to Portugal, around 409, had founded a city—this same city of Luna. But that knowledge was of no use to him. He grasped it with his intellect. His emotions, however, could not rid themselves of the idea that the city was named for the moon, and the Don Alvaro de Luna, the father of the Bastard, was the ancestor of a long series of moon people.

The lamp, whose shade was dark green outside and white inside, cast a strong light on the Coello atlas; and just as the moon receives and throws back the light of the sun, so the moon landscape on the map seemed to transform the white sheen of the lamp into silver moonlight and to cast it back onto the shadowed face of the observer. At the same time, the shores of the Bay of Barcelona and the Gulf of Biscay kept reminding him of the stony curves of the Sea of Darkness and the Sea of Rain, and the Pyrenees more and more seemed to suggest a mountain range of stellar iron. If one looked at it long enough, Jessiersky thought, one would become a moonstruck sleepwalker. Saturated with the light of this landscape, one might later—so he thought—feel impelled to get up out of bed without waking up, cross the rooms and walk up the stairs, tap, tap, to the loft. Then, as is the way of sleepwalkers, one might step out onto the roof through one of the attic windows and, without knowing what one was doing— blind to all dangers—take a stroll on the roof....

Curiously enough, he now seemed really to hear the tapping of the footsteps which he had been imagining. But after a few moments, he realized that these were real sounds and that he must also have heard them before on preceding nights. Only then he had not paid any attention to them. But he *had* heard them, and now he was hearing them again.

The tapping did not come from the floor immediately above the library, not from the next floor, but from the one above that which was a kind of attic. Throughout the house and even in the street, it was so still at this time of night that, although the sound was far away and very soft, one not only could hear it distinctly, but also could tell exactly where it was coming from. The steps were coming, tonight at any rate, from the back of the house, from the direction of the narrow street which ran behind the house. They passed over the two library rooms, the dining room, and the big parlors and started down the stairs leading to the door that gave onto Bankgasse. The crystal chandeliers on the ceiling over which the footsteps passed jingled slightly. It was as though a man in armor were walking about overhead.

On the floor between the one on which the library was located and the one on which he had heard the steps were the bedrooms of the family. But neither the footfalls nor the vibration that caused the jingling of the chandeliers came from there. Both came from the floor above where the servants were sleeping, or rather were not sleeping, since if they were sleeping they would scarcely be tapping about in the night! It might be the footman who was paying a visit to the cook, or the chauffeur who had felt obliged to pay his respects to the governess. But what did that matter? Was Jessiersky supposed to be his servants' keeper? He did decide, however, to forbid this tapping about. After all, it was half past two.

He rose, left the library, crossed the parlor, and had just reached the door that opened onto the stairway when he realized that the tapping individual had not only walked down the stairs, but already passed the door behind which he, Jessiersky, was standing.

The fellow now must have reached the front hall, for Jessiersky could hear the glass door that closed off the stairwell being shut. The nocturnal wanderer, who, up to now, had moved in a fairly leisurely fashion, must suddenly have dashed down the dark stairs as fast as he could.

Jessiersky, who had stepped out onto the landing, did not take the time to consider whether it had been he, or something else, that had caused the sudden flight. He turned on the light in the stairwell and ran down the steps. But the very moment he came to the glass door and entered the front hall, one of the wings of the heavy entrance door, which, meanwhile, must have been unlocked and opened, was being closed again from the outside. He was just about to fling it open and dash after the fugitive when he thought better of it. He switched off the light and cautiously opened a hand's breadth the wing which had been left unlocked.

The night was restless with fitful gusts of wind. The sky, a bit of which could be seen above the Ballhausplatz, was covered with a web of moonlit clouds. The wind was gentle and warm for the season. The lights of the street lamps stretching from the Liechtenstein Palace to the Dietrichstein Palace flickered, much like a swarm of will-o'-the-wisps, in the deep shadows of the buildings. But there was no human being in sight.

Jessiersky peered up and down the street which was dotted with puddles of melted snow. He could hear the far-off roar of a few late trucks. The tangled masses of bare trees in the nearby public gardens looked like huge brambles, and farther off, the iron chariots with their teams of four horses on the roof of the parliament buildings stood out against the moonlit clouds drifting in the southerly breeze.

After looking about for a while, Jessiersky went over to the Hungarian Embassy and inquired of the policeman who was on duty there whether he had seen anyone leave the Strattmann Palace. No one but him, the policeman replied. But when Jessiersky had thanked the man and started back, he thought he saw a shadowy figure slip out of the door of his house and scurry off in the direction of the Burgtheater. Jessiersky immediately began to run after the figure. But no sooner had he made the first steps than the shadow vanished.

Chapter 6

It was hardly surprising that the male and female servants should sometimes visit each other. The prelude to such calls always followed the same, or much the same, pattern. One of the girls, as she was ironing, perhaps, would begin to sing a sentimental song: "Do you remember the hour ..." for instance, or "A woman lay down, God wanted it thus...." Then the men would know that the time was ripe. And the footman, the chauffeur, or the doorman (a married man with adulterous leanings), after studying the curves of the ironing songstress for a while, would come up to her—always in the same atavistic fashion—from behind. He would address her as "Fräulein" and inquire about her home and family, although he had not the faintest interest in them. Finally, if it happened to be summer, he would propose an outing in the Prater for the following Sunday, or if it were winter, he would suggest that they go to the movies. That, too, was always the same, for they could afford nothing else. After a time, the couple would decide that they could be far more comfortable at home than in the seats of a movie theater, or in the damp grass, surrounded by gnats. So they simply made themselves more comfortable at home....

So much for the visits within the household. There were, of course, also others, from people who did not belong to the household; obviously this caller had been one of *them*. But where and how had he got the house key or a duplicate of it? Which of the maids had had it made and given it to her lover? Or had the entrance door been left unlocked? Here Jessiersky caught his breath, and beads of perspiration formed on his forehead as he realized that with the door unlocked at night … But that was what came of spending all that time in the library and never thinking to check the door!

From that moment on, he could not get rid of the thought that the nocturnal visitor might not have been simply an admirer of his wife's chambermaid or of the young kitchen help, but someone else altogether. He was not sure it would be wise to question the staff; the night visitor, having got wind of Jessiersky's inquiries, would merely exercise greater caution!

Finally Jessiersky decided to sound the servants out after all. It occurred to him that they, too, might have heard something and might have some further information to offer. Of course, they would offer it only if they too had merely *heard* the visitor. If, on the other hand, one of the women had a personal interest in him, that is, if she had been visited by him, his nocturnal presence in the building could be dismissed as harmless anyway—unless he had called on her only for the purpose of getting into the house. Except for that alternative, then, Jessiersky could assume the visit to have been of a not innocuous kind only if every single one of the servants, of the females, at least, declared that she had heard the steps. The word of the female servants was important because an outside woman was most unlikely to call on one of the male domestics at night. Therefore, *one* woman who, in order not to give herself away, would say nothing about the footfalls could be considered proof of the harmlessness of the visitor. But the questioning would have to be handled with great tact. And how, even with the most tactful approach, would the servants be able to make statements, if most of them, perhaps all of them, had been asleep and had not been able to hear anything?

Jessiersky became aware that the moment he felt himself again threatened with Luna's presence, his thoughts began to turn in a circle. In fact, they grew confused. So for instance he could not resist the impulse to make a series of "calculations." Had Luna been present at regular or irregular intervals? And if the intervals had been regular, how long had they been? That Jessiersky should embark upon such "calculations" was not in itself particularly disquieting. What was disquieting was that he then tried to ascertain whether the intervals between Luna's visits were divisible by the length of the period from one full moon to the next, or by the duration of one phase of the moon.

Just as the moon was supposed to influence the weather, so Luna undoubtedly had an influence upon the climate of events! And there must be times, so Jessiersky came to feel, when Luna's command over the forces which enabled him to deceive, to inflict harm, perhaps even to kill, was greater than usual, and times when he was practically powerless. But during the intervening period, it was prescribed that he should grow and diminish in power at a regular rate. Every night and every day he rose and set and controlled the ebb and flow of events which concerned him. It was also quite possible that his own physiognomy waxed and waned, his crescent-moon-shaped face with the prominent forehead and chin and the rather pushed-in features in the middle, his skin with its pock-like blemishes which looked like volcano craters; his entire body, indeed, might grow sturdier or frailer at regular intervals. The picture at the Millemoths', for instance, in which he looked strikingly thin, might have been taken at a time when it was, so to speak, new moon with him. A fortnight later, however, he would certainly have looked far more robust. In short, he had phases, phases like the moon....

Cursing the absurdity of such thoughts, Jessiersky tore up the paper on which he had set down his calculations, rang the bell, and gave the order for the entire domestic staff to appear at once.

To sum up briefly, the questioning, although Jessiersky conducted it, or tried to conduct it, with the utmost tact, produced no results. This was largely due to Elisabeth Jessiersky who came in with the staff and kept throwing in such questions as: What was all this excitement about? what was this about footsteps having been heard at night? who in the world could it have been? and so forth. The servants, flustered by her undisciplined questions, began to reply in an equally undisciplined fashion, the most undisciplined aspect of their behavior being that their answers took the form of questions. Who did Herr Jessiersky think they were? Had they ever given him any reason to assume that the servant floor was a den of iniquity? Did he really think that after all the heavy work during the day they had nothing better to do than to flit about the rooms all night? If the nocturnal visitor—as Jessiersky has said himself—had escaped, it was clear that he, not they, was to blame for the disturbance. So they asked him in all deference to refrain from casting any further suspicion on them. It would never have been possible to make any such accusations in the first place, they went on, if domestic help were unionized! Incidentally, they had been meaning to tell him that hours were too long, not to speak of the free afternoons they had coming to them.... And so it went on for a considerable time. Finally the cook gave notice.

Very soon after the servants had started to speak, Alexander Jessiersky fell silent and stared at them thoughtfully. Again, as at the time of the Third Reich, he had the uneasy feeling of belonging to an extremely thin stratum of humanity which had not the most remote realization of what was going on in the strata beneath. The cook, for instance, who had just given notice, was a so-called master cook; but under certain circumstances, this

66

fact—so Jessiersky imagined—would not have deterred her for a moment from using her knife on her employers. That the man-servant who waited on Jessiersky every day had not long since struck him dead with the bootjack could be attributed only to the fact that, had he done so, he would have been out of a job....

Snapping out of his bewilderment at last, Jessiersky chased everyone, including his wife, out of the room. This had not been the way to go about it. There was nothing, it seemed, that was important enough to distract people from their preoccupation with their own trivial concerns; and inasmuch as the questioning had started off in the direction of the absurd, nothing and nobody could have steered it back onto the track of reason anyway. Jessiersky might well consider himself lucky if all this fuss had not made the nocturnal caller as wary as a frightened roebuck and never appear again.

This, apparently, was exactly what happened. For weeks, even months, the sinister prowler gave no sign of life, and Jessiersky lay in wait for him in vain. It might have been supposed that Jessiersky, having frightened away, or seemingly frightened away, the fellow, had accomplished his purpose. But his intention had not been so much to scare him off as to find out who he was. For while he could have sworn that it was Luna, he had been unable to prove it to himself.

He tried, at least, to discover what Luna, if it really had been Luna, might have been doing in the house. He scoured it from top to bottom for traces of his ghostly adversary. He then attempted to discover, not what Luna had done, but what he might have done if he had not been frightened away prematurely. Conceivably, he might have tried to do something to the next youngest again, since his plot on her life the preceding year had failed. But the child had long since recovered and showed no signs of falling ill again. Moreover, all the rest of the family were enjoying the best of health. This should have set Jessiersky's mind at ease. But at this point he began to wonder whether he cared very much about his family. He cared about Luna, he realized, far more than about his family.

It was toward the end of January that Jessiersky had heard the tapping, and until far into April, he waited for Luna night after night, never closing his eyes before the break of day. Then he would sleep until two or three in the afternoon and between five and seven in the evening would—occasionally—go to his office. The directors were surprised that Jessiersky took so little interest in the business; and his wife was secretly amazed when he went to bed at ten or, at the latest, eleven in the evening and then stayed there until the following afternoon. But on the whole, this behavior harmed neither his household nor his business.

For his business continued to prosper, partly due to the continued tension in the international situation. The idea that international tensions had a depressing effect upon business was an obsolete notion. In reality, more money was made because of the tensions. But Jessiersky had not the slightest interest in this kind of tension. The strain of his own life was quite enough for him. In fact, it was fast becoming too much for him and he could stand it no longer. Simply in order to make something happen, no matter how pointless, he resolved to look up the Millemoths once again.

He could have taken the car. But this time, too, he went on foot, as though he were going on a forbidden errand as in the days of the Third Reich. On leaving his house, he had a distinct feeling that he was being watched. Only now it was not the agents of the Third Reich he suspected of being interested in his doings; he felt that he was being shadowed by Luna—a threat more sinister still.

It was a Friday afternoon and the traffic was unusually great.

There was an air of frenzy about it, for everyone was hurrying to wind up his business as quickly as possible to get off for the weekend. It was not so much the roar of the cars and trucks and motorcycles that got on Jessiersky's nerves as the idea that he could be watched from all these vehicles without knowing whose eye was focused upon him. It seemed to him that there were thousands of eyes. The countless motorcycles, in particular, made him feel as though he were surrounded with a buzzing swarm of unearthly insects. The people on the motorcycles, ostensibly quite harmless businessmen, engineers, and workmen, were like spies in disguise who kept circling about him.

There was no response when Jessiersky rang the doorbell of the Millemoth apartment. He learned from the janitor that they were out of town.

"Where did they go?" he asked, outwardly calm, inwardly controlling an urge to box the fellow's ears in place of those of the departed Millemoths.

To Deutsch-Altenburg, the janitor told him, where Frau Millemoth was taking the baths.

"Is that so?" said Jessiersky. "What kind of baths? What for, or rather why does she need them?"

That he could not exactly say, answered the janitor. And unfortunately the Millemoths' tenant, who might have been able to give him more details, seemed not to be at home.

"Herr Berdiczewer?" Jessiersky asked, trying to recall the story the Millemoths had told him about the man.

No, that one, thank God, had departed. The janitor, who at the time of the Third Reich had been a good party man, then went on to inform him that a Sudeten German was living with the Millemoths now, a man by the name of Perwein, a very fine fellow indeed. And as he began to list his fine qualities, Jessiersky wondered whether the Millemoths, and Luna, too—in particular, Luna—had not seemed at least as suspicious to this janitor as Herr Berdiczewer. "But Count Luna," Jessiersky said, while he took out his wallet to tip the janitor, "doesn't he also live with Herr and Frau Millemoth?"

"Oh, my God," said the janitor, taking the tip, "our Count Luna! That's quite some time ago, I'm sorry to say...." He waved his hand in a gesture of regret.

"But doesn't he come to call from time to time?" asked Jessiersky, watching the janitor closely.

"To call?" exclaimed the janitor in amazement. "But how could he? From where?"

Jessiersky did not answer at once. Finally he said: "And Herr and Frau Millemoth, you say, are in Deutsch-Altenburg?"

"Yes, that's correct," said the janitor.

Jessiersky studied his expression for a moment longer, then inquired where he could make a telephone call.

Two houses down there was a telephone booth, the janitor told him.

Jessiersky hurriedly said good-bye and left the building. The janitor looked after him uneasily.

From the telephone booth, Jessiersky called his house and ordered the car to be brought to him.

The chauffeur drove up in the car ten minutes later. Jessiersky sent him home and then, seating himself at the wheel, set off for Deutsch-Altenburg.

Just beyond Schwechat, the flat countryside around him began to spread out in the light of the sinking sun. To the left there were a series of wooded terraces sloping down toward the Danube and continuing on out of sight beyond the river into the Marchfeld. On the right, though far in the distance, the land was bounded by a low range of mountains. Gray cloud islands with luminous red towers rising up from them floated on the horizon.

In Maria Ellend, a village between Fischamend and Petronell, he came around a curve just as an oncoming truck was rounding it from the opposite direction. Suddenly a motorcycle with two peasant boys appeared directly in front of him. The driver, who was trying to pass the truck, had become blinded by the light of the setting sun and was about to crash head on into Jessiersky's car. Jessiersky quickly pulled the machine as far as he could over to the right, with the result that the motorcycle struck his car somewhere close to the left front wheel, shot up high in the air, its wheels still spinning, and then fell to the ground back of the car. The motorcycle driver was hurled against the windshield of the automobile, and the sidecar passenger thrown across the top; Jessiersky's car, after rolling over the shallow macadamized ditch of the highway and mowing down one of the sparse acacias in front of a house, came to a standstill.

Jessiersky shook off the glass splinters he had been showered with and climbed out of the car. A number of people came running to see what had happened, and the passing cars drew up along the curb. The two motorcyclists were obviously seriously injured. One of them was lying motionless on his back like a dead frog; the other, with his hands over his face, was rolling on the ground, screaming with pain. Jessiersky's face, neck, and wrists were bleeding from many tiny wounds caused by the glass splinters. The radiator of his car was smashed in and the chassis was also undoubtedly bent. Only the motorcycle itself was practically unhurt.

The crowd immediately blamed Jessiersky for the accident although—or, perhaps, just because—it had quite obviously been the fault of the cyclists. He, therefore, hurriedly called up his lawyer in Vienna and asked him to come at once to the scene of the accident. The lawyer appeared after three-quarters of an hour, but by that time it was dark. The cyclists had been taken into one of the houses. Jessiersky had been bandaged up by the local doctor who had not failed to advise him to drive a little more carefully the next time. The police had already been functioning for a considerable while by the light of the headlights of Jessiersky's car as well as with their flashlights. Later a fair copy of the report was made in the village inn, and an ambulance appeared to take the motorcyclists to the hospital.

Jessiersky left his car behind in the village. He had tried to drive it, but it clattered like a coffee mill, and he had discovered that, on top of everything else, the axle was bent.

He returned to Vienna with his lawyer and discussed the matter with him at length for another hour. He was angry because the police, as well as the inhabitants of Maria Ellend, had sided with the motorcyclists.

"That surprises you?" asked the lawyer. "I would have been surprised if they hadn't."

"Now the last straw," said Jessiersky, "would be if the court should be against me." His plan to call on the Millemoths was all but forgotten. For the moment he was thinking neither of the nocturnal visits at the Strattmann Palace nor of the possibility that the unknown caller might be Luna. All this had simply gone out of his mind.

When he arrived home, it was already past midnight and the house was completely dark. He unlocked the entrance door, went straight to his dressing room, and looked at himself in the mirror. Despite the bitter resentment seething within him, he could not help laughing. He face was dotted with bits of adhesive tape. He lighted a cigarette and blew the smoke against the mirror. Then it occurred to him again that the collision might cost him a pretty penny, particularly if one of the motorcyclists should die. For then this person, dead as he was, would rise up and attack him, just as Luna, dead as he himself had assumed him to be, had already risen up to attack him.

At this moment he again heard the footfalls.

But this time he heard them not from two stories up—as he had in the library, months before—but from the next floor, the one just above. And again, they came from the back of the house, passed over his head, and turned down the stairs. The chandeliers over which the steps passed jingled much more clearly this time. For here, on the third floor, the chandeliers were not made of crystal, as they were on the second. Both Jessiersky's dressing room and his bedroom had metal chandeliers; and the jingling was no longer the jingling of glass; it had a metallic ring—as though a man in armor were walking through the house. There was an armed man up there, and since he wore armor, it must be Luna, for who else would wear armor here? Surely not a lover of the chambermaid, or an admirer of the scullery maid! Indeed, Luna, though related to the wretched Millemoths, did not hesitate to face danger! After all, he was a descendant of the Count de Gormas and of the Portuguese Infanta. He was a Knight of Malta, and because he might have to do battle when he came here, he had put on a complete suit of armor, such as the Knights had worn when Valencia was sacked, or Rhodes was lost under the Grand Master Villiers de l'Isle Adam. His spurs had a golden ring ... and a pale glow shimmered like moonlight about him....

Unconscious of the absurdity of his imaginings, Jessiersky began to search about madly for a weapon, any sort of instrument, any object with which he could attack Luna and throw him down. But there were no longer any weapons in the house. (They had all been turned in when the city was taken, since, quite understandably, the Allies wished to misbehave with as little danger to themselves as possible.) By the time the man had reached the stairwell and the sound of the steps was already beginning to fade into the distance, Jessiersky had found nothing better with which to arm himself than a pair of scissors that were lying on his dressing table. It was the biggest of a half dozen, about six inches long. But as a weapon, especially as a weapon with which to attack a man in full armor, it was utterly ridiculous. How could he have watched and waited for months, and, now that Luna had finally come, have nothing with which to meet him but a pair of scissors! He ran through the two parlors and was just about to fling open the door onto the stairway when he had the sense to realize that it would be extremely foolish to stage a struggle—and probably a fatal one—with so dreadful an adversary right in the house. Although his heart was in his mouth, he prevailed upon himself to wait by the door until Luna's footsteps—still clinking metallically, as Jessiersky imagined—had descended the staircase and passed by the door. He seemed to hear the edges of the pieces of armor softly rubbing against one another as the man went on down the stairs.

Finally Jessiersky opened the door. Luna had walked down in the dark, and Jessiersky did not switch on the light. Tightly clutching the scissors, he too followed in darkness. He heard Luna open and close the glass door at the bottom of the stairs, then unlock the entrance door, step out onto the street, and lock both wings again from the outside. The other time, he had, in his haste, left one wing unlocked; this time he obviously had no suspicion that anyone might be following him. Now Jessiersky also hurried down the staircase and across the hall. When he had unlocked the door and reached the street, he could still see Luna over toward the Burgtheater, just disappearing, like a shadow, around the corner of Bankgasse.

As he began to run after him, he told himself that it was madness to try to attack a deadly enemy with a pair of scissors. But he knew that he would have assaulted him even with his bare hands. Meanwhile, Luna had walked past the rear of the Burgtheater and had turned onto Teinfaltstrasse. His footsteps, although out of doors they no longer sounded metallic, or even like crystal, echoed in the stillness of the night. By the light of the street lamps, Jessiersky now saw clearly that Luna was not wearing armor—it had been ridiculous to think he was wearing armor and was clothed in rattling mail. Jessiersky was following him at a distance of less than a hundred steps, and he began to wonder how he could catch up with Luna without attracting his attention. For now was the moment to do so—the street was deserted....

Luna, to his misfortune, stopped to light a cigarette. Instantly Jessiersky ran up to him on tiptoe and threw himself upon him. Luna, taken completely by surprise, fell forward on his face. Jessiersky, blind with rage, the scissors clutched in his hand, jabbed them again and again, like a knife, into the nape of Luna's neck. His victim began to emit horrible, choking cries of despair and even managed to raise himself up for a moment to shove Jessiersky away. But he flopped down almost at once, rolled over and over, and finally lay motionless.

Jessiersky, who had flattened himself out against the wall of a house, peered up and down the street but could see nothing. His heart was pounding loudly, in frightful agitation. Then as though the wind on the ocean of his soul had suddenly shifted, a kind of pity swept over him for the miserable death of this man whose joyless, cramped existence, with the many years spent in prison camps and then in the darkness of the underworld and of anonymity, had all ended now in this hopeless struggle for breath, in this awful choking in his own blood.

At last Jessiersky ventured to approach the prostrate figure.

Luna was lying in a puddle. A long rivulet of blood was trickling across the sidewalk and into the street. It looked as if a dog had relieved itself beside Luna's head.

When Jessiersky turned over the body, however, in order to get a good look at the pockmarked face with the pushed-in features that he had so often imagined, he saw that this man whom he had killed, in order to kill Luna, was not Luna. It was Baron Spinette, whom he knew slightly, a distant cousin of Elisabeth Jessiersky.

Chapter 7

He gently lifted the dead man's head and held it in his hands. There was something strangely repugnant about holding in one's hand the still warm, but already lifeless head of a man as one might hold the living head of a child or a woman. After a few seconds, he let the head fall back onto the pavement and quickly searched the man's pockets for the key to the Strattmann house. When he found it, he got to his feet, looked all around, and listened. Everything was still quiet in the street. The only sound was the far off hum of city traffic. The lamps above the center of the street were swaying gently in the night wind, and the light was flitting back and forth across the asphalt as though ghostly birds were fluttering about the lamps.

Jessiersky went back by the same way he had come only a few minutes before, following hard on the heels of his victim. As he walked along, he wrapped up his right hand in a handkerchief. When he reached the house, he found the door unlocked just as he had left it. He pushed open one wing with his handkerchiefed hand, turned the key which was still sticking in the inside lock, and hurried up the stairs. In his bathroom he washed his hands. Then he went into the dressing room, emptied his pockets, and took off his suit and underwear. He put the handkerchief and scissors with the clothes and rolled them up, wrapped the bundle in a newspaper, and tied it with twine which, after some searching, he had found in a drawer. Then he returned to the bathroom, washed his whole body thoroughly, put on fresh underwear and another suit, and left the house, the bundle under his arm.

Whether the policeman who was stationed in front of the Hungarian Embassy noticed him—whether, in fact, he had noticed his previous departure and return—was impossible to tell. Jessiersky turned right and hastily made his way toward the Ringstrasse. There he picked up a taxicab, whose driver, staring at Jessiersky's face with all the adhesive tape on it, did not look at the parcel. Jessiersky had the taxi take him to the quay of the Danube Canal. At the corner of Rotenturmstrasse he left the cab and continued on, bundle in hand, to the bridge, and from there, at a moment when he thought no one was watching him, he tossed the package into the water.

Then he started returning home on foot. Only now, when he thought he had washed off all traces of his deed, had got rid of all the objects that might have given him away, did he begin to consider the dreadful consequences of the mistaken identity. But had it really been a case of mistaken identity? Yes and no. For it was clear to Jessiersky that his wife had betrayed him, that she had received her cousin in one of the guest rooms on the top floor instead of in her own bedroom where Jessiersky might walk in at any moment. But Jessiersky asked himself whether her unfaithfulness alone would have prompted him to do what he had done to Spinette. Scarcely. There had been a time—and he himself had heard tales about it as a child—when such things were done. Back in those days, every other week or so, some officer would stab one of his rivals in a wardrobe or behind the bedroom stove, where the poor man had taken refuge. It was also said that quite often in the Army Riding Instructors' Academy when the trainers went into the covered ring in the morning, they would find a pool of blood left from some duel which had just taken place. But nowadays no one bothered to go to all that trouble.

A man simply threw his wife out. Or he might not even go that far and just let her do as she pleased. Jessiersky was also aware that for years he had grossly neglected his wife, although the last thing she wanted was to be neglected. In short, he could not help admitting to himself that he had killed Spinette only because he had taken him for Luna, and that otherwise, he surely would not have murdered him. At the same time he was convinced that he ought to have killed Spinette in any case; it was quite possible that other people, real businessmen, simply threw out the wives who betrayed them and sometimes did not even go that far; but he, Jessiersky, who was not a real businessman, had killed his wife's lover. And because he was, as he believed, perfectly justified in killing him, Jessiersky experienced no pangs of conscience.

For Spinette may not even have been Elisabeth Jessiersky's only lover. That fellow, for instance, whose steps he had heard in the winter had not necessarily been Spinette. He might have been someone else entirely. Perhaps, in addition to these two, this one and the one the past winter, she had had a third, or even a fourth, lover. But however many there may have been, one of them was out now, and that might make all of them a little less impetuous.

And Luna? From all appearances, he did not want to risk a personal encounter with Jessiersky. But might it not have been he after all who had got Jessiersky embroiled in this murder? This was not unlikely … in fact it was quite likely, for he would scarcely have merely wanted to do him the favor of pointing out to him that his wife had a lover. Instead, he had got Jessiersky into a situation in which he would now have to be extremely careful if he did not want the devil to get him. Jessiersky did not stop to consider that the whole affair might have nothing to do with Luna. The connection between Luna and Spinette was perfectly obvious! Why else would he, Jessiersky, obsessed with his fear of Luna and the desire to get rid of him, have neglected his wife to such an extent that she had finally turned to other men? Luna had failed in his scheme of bringing misfortune upon one of the children after the other. On his first attempt to poison the next youngest, he had come to grief. So he had concentrated on Jessiersky himself, attacking him through his wife. In Jessiersky's eyes, Luna was a more or less ghostly madman who had returned from the realm of the dead, as it were, solely for the purpose of retaliation—an avenger lifted into the sphere of a higher conscience who did not and would not understand that Jessiersky was not to blame for his misfortune; and Jessiersky no longer doubted that such a person was capable of establishing relations that had nothing to do with reason, and that, therefore, would have consequences far more logical and more frightful than those of any scheme devised by reason.

When he reached home, dawn was already beginning to break. The policeman in front of the Hungarian Embassy took no notice of him, as far as he could tell, and it was also possible that, during the interval, there might have been a change of guards. Jessiersky unlocked the door for the third time that night, walked up the stairs to his bedroom, and went to bed. But he could not sleep. It was as though the dawn had entered the house with him, for a gray light, like a cobweb, hung over all the furniture, all the objects in the room. It grew brighter and brighter, and instead of obliterating the images that were flooding his mind, it made them more sharply defined—as though they were projected right there before him in the room. He kept seeing Spinette, feeling him, as he had tried to raise himself up, tried to shake him off, to throw him off. He kept hearing the pitiful, choking cry of the unfortunate man; and it sounded and sounded in his ear like an electric bell that has got stuck.

It was now broad daylight, but still he had not slept. He heard the bells of the Minorite Church and of St. Michael's, the morning sounds in the house, and the distant noise of the street. The hours crept by, but still he did not get up. This time, too, though there was no longer any reason for it, he stayed in bed until three in the afternoon.

Finally he got up, drove to his office, which on this Saturday afternoon was completely empty, and there he read the midday papers. They not only mentioned his collision with the two motorcyclists in Maria Ellend, but also contained a full report of Spinette's death. It was thought to be a robbery murder committed by a particularly bestial killer. For the dead man had no less than twenty-two wounds in his neck, his head, and his back, "apparently made by a dull pocket knife," and in his pockets, except for a little change, there was nothing of value. Jessiersky laughed aloud. Of course there was nothing of value in Spinette's pockets! For a long time, there had been nothing of value in those pockets. Ever since the dowry of Jessiersky's wife, Hradek and Sossnowetz, had been taken away from him, Jessiersky hated all aristocrats who had also had everything taken away from them. He thought it absurd that the dispossessed should still be going about with titles when they could no longer command the price of a streetcar ride.

That evening at dinner, Elisabeth Jessiersky was still so overcome with emotion that she could not even bring herself to comment on her husband's motor accident. But she did her best to control herself. He looked at her closely—for the first time in a long while. She was now thirty-five, but despite all the children she had had, she did not look more than twenty-eight, thirty, at most. It occurred to him that she had never lost her girlish looks. . . . But did she really believe that her cousin had been killed by a robber? "She should be able to guess the truth," Jessiersky told himself, "—guess it by mistake, for she may well suppose that I got my face all scratched up in a fight with her lover. Otherwise she would not be making such an effort to control herself— why should she? And surely she would make some allusion to the murder, instead of not saying a word about it." At last he said to her: "I am sorry to hear that your cousin ... on the street ... very strange, right here in our neighborhood!"

"Yes," she stammered, looking at him with the eyes of a frightened heifer, "so you, too, find it odd that it happened here."

What else could she say? thought Jessiersky. She might even think that he would be trying to kill her next. "Really," he said to himself, "no matter how reasonable people may think they are, the moment their so-called passions get involved, they become completely witless."

He continued to follow everything that was published in the papers concerning Spinette's death and very shortly he became convinced that the real murderer would never be discovered. The police picked up their old customers—those fellows with whom crime had become such a habit they committed it rather carelessly. Their pictures were in the rogues' gallery at headquarters, where that collection was genteelly referred to as the "Albums"— like the volumes of family photographs on the parlor tables of the eighties—and the police had only to look through them to pick up suspects. The police, after all, were only human, or rather, only officials, who like all officials, disliked nothing so much as to be put to extra trouble. If a person had managed to avoid getting his photograph into one of those "Albums," he could do anything he wanted, within what he chose to regard as reasonable limits.

Jessiersky went with his wife to Spinette's funeral as though he were simply paying his last respects to a man who had not had an affair with his wife and whom he had not killed on account of this affair. After the funeral the police still did not appear at the house, but only Spinette's mother. She and her son had lived on a meager pension from her late husband, a civil servant, and she now assumed that the rich Jessierskys would pay for the funeral expenses, at least. Alexander Jessiersky was on the point of telling her that now that her son was gone, she would have more to spend on herself. But he refrained from making this remark and merely gave the now slightly more prosperous baroness a look of disgust, and paid for the funeral.

"This tragic event," he said to his wife, "has not only upset you, but also disturbed me, as I notice. I, therefore, suggest that we go to Zinkeneck earlier than usual this year. Take the children out of school, or leave them here, if you want, with the governess. But be ready yourself to go with me in a few days."

She tried to say something in reply, but could only move her lips.

It would have done her no good to raise any objections, for, meanwhile, some very good reasons for going to the country at once had presented themselves to Jessiersky's mind. In the city, it seemed to him, he really was at the mercy of his sinister persecutor: it was so easy for the man to lose himself in this impenetrable human thicket, to leap out at him from the crowd and vanish at will. While in the country, particularly in Zinkeneck, where Jessiersky knew his way about reasonably well—and in the countryside generally, which was virtually empty of people—he would certainly notice anything that was going on and would know it if anyone tried to get near him. In the city, for example, the affair between Elisabeth and Spinette had probably gone on for months without attracting any attention. Such a thing would be impossible in the country! Spinette would only have had to stop at the village inn, or at the one in the neighboring village, to become the talk of the whole valley; it would have been impossible for him to get into the house at night without being bitten by the dogs; and if he had tried to meet Elisabeth somewhere outside the house, it would have created a scandal overnight. What applied to Spinette applied to an even greater degree to Luna, and Jessiersky could not remember, in fact, ever having seen any sign of him in Zinkeneck. He had shown himself only in Vienna. Therefore Jessiersky and his family would be quite safe there, for Luna, if he dared to come at all, would be completely at his mercy.

But two days later Elisabeth announced that the schools had refused to let the children go so early. The children, therefore, would have to stay with Mademoiselle, and it might, after all, be best if the two of them ...

Why, wondered Jessiersky, is she so set against going to the country? Aloud he said, "Not at all, my dear! We are leaving, and your offspring, whether the stupid schools want them to go or not, will leave with us."

"But you said ..."

"Yes—but now I've changed my mind. Pack your things and be quick about it."

Chapter 8

Zinkeneck was situated at a point in the high mountains where four valleys met, or rather, where two side valleys came into a main valley. And as they together formed the shape of a cross, and as each of them had a mountain brook flowing through it, Jessiersky had named the rivulets after the rivers of Paradise. There, to be sure, it was the sources of the streams that were adjacent to one another, while here it was the mouths; and Paradise had four rivers while here there were merely three brooks. But he solved the problem by naming the main brook, upward from the point at which the side brooks flowed into it, Gihon, and the section below, Pison. The right-hand tributary he called Euphrates, and the left one, Hiddekel. But he frequently mixed up the names; and his gamekeepers, not only because of that curious nomenclature, but for other reasons as well, thought Jessiersky insane.

Originally, the name Zinkeneck was not applied to the village, but to a mountain rising from the spur of a much higher mountain that was situated between Hiddekel and Gihon and was called Hochzinken. *Zinken* means "to shine"; *Zinken* are also certain stringed instruments with a high, bright tone; and finally, country people refer to a red, shiny nose as a *Zinken*. Zinkeneck, then, literally means the Village at the Foot of the Spur of a High Shiny Mountain. It had been originally made up of the farm buildings belonging to the "castle," a stone hunting lodge built by Emperor Maximilian I. That castle, together with the hunting preserve, had been purchased by old Fries about the turn of the century—God knows why, for surely he had never been cut out for hunting in the high mountains. Probably he had made this purchase, as well as that of the Strattmann Palace, to give prestige to the firm. His grandson, however, accepted with grace not only the palace but also the estate, and when anyone inquired how long it had been in the possession of the family, would reply scornfully, "For three generations now."

The castle was reached from the village by crossing a beautiful old stone bridge over the Pison. The structure stood in the angle formed by Pison and Hiddekel—in other words, in the region of the heart of an imagined huge man suspended on the cross formed by the brooks. The village then was situated in the region of his liver, extending on for a little distance (across the Euphrates) into the region of the right lung of the giant. In the region of his left lung, that is, in the angle between Gihon and Hiddekel and right at the foot of the Hochzinken, lay the park of the castle, which Jessiersky had named the "Garden of Eden" although—or perhaps because—owing to the high altitude, it had never done very well; since the three dry summers immediately following the war, it had consisted mostly of windblown trees, among them a rather tall and particularly windblown one—the "Tree of the Knowledge of Good and Evil," as Jessiersky called it. But it was in the inhabitants of the village that he saw the most striking similarity to conditions in Paradise, or, more correctly, to conditions prevailing there at a certain moment. In the eyes of Jessiersky, who had been forced to deal with those people for decades, their depravity was quite comparable to that of our first ancestors after the fall. Had it been possible for him to drive them out, he gladly would have done so. But he had neither the power nor the means.

The castle, or hunting lodge, was built of quarry stone, but the door jambs and window frames were of marble. Above the entrance was a plaque with the coat of arms of Maximilian, disproportionately large for the size of the house. On it, the imperial eagle surrounded with its wings a huge cross on which was the figure of Christ. Nestling between the arms of the cross were the shields of all the countries over which the Emperor had ruled. Twined around the cross and the shields was a chain from which was suspended the Golden Fleece.

The mountain world all around was tremendously imposing. The wind from the high peaks was constantly beating against the last vestiges of a primeval forest which was still attempting to climb the slope but was making little headway. As a general rule, it was possible to live quite comfortably here for a few months of every summer. Elisabeth Jessiersky, however, this year was of another opinion. For after only six weeks she became so ill that the doctor from Schreinbach, the next community, which was slightly larger than Zinkeneck, held out no hope for her recovery. A specialist Jessiersky then sent for from the capital of the province was in agreement with the village doctor. For, said he, when a lady had herself operated upon illegally, she should at least see to it that it was not performed in a manner bound to result in blood poisoning.

Blood poisoning seemed to be Luna's specialty. His plans had misfired in the case of the next youngest. But now, in the case of Elisabeth Jessiersky, he had carried them out! Though Alexander Jessiersky told himself again and again that it was the Zinkeneck midwife who had performed the operation because there had been no time for it in Vienna who was to blame for his wife's death, the person really to blame was Luna. Had it not been for Luna, Jessiersky himself, not Spinette, would have been the father of Elisabeth's child. But because Spinette had been its father, it had not been allowed to come into the world and had cost its mother her life. That was why she had not wanted to leave Vienna! And if it had not been for Luna, Jessiersky would not have gone so early to Zinkeneck. But he had gone because of him, and now his wife was dying.

She followed the unborn child and his father down into the darkness, and while she was still on her deathbed, he thought back over the first years of his marriage with her, of the time when she still owned Hradek and Sossnowetz, when everything had been different. And if in the end she had betrayed him, it was not her fault, or, at least, not entirely her fault. It was really he, Jessiersky himself, or rather Luna, again, who was to blame; and that was why he was sorry for his wife, as he had been sorry for Spinette.

All this took place at the beginning of August. Several of Elisabeth's relatives appeared for the funeral; as they were titled, they had been forced to flee from Czechoslovakia and were quite penniless. Jessiersky disliked them immensely. And although Elisabeth's father and brother were also present (her mother, whose dowry, Sossnowetz and Hradek, Elisabeth had inherited and brought to her own marriage, had been dead for some time), Jessiersky spoke as little as possible with any of them. It was his privilege to be speechless with grief, and he took the fullest possible advantage of it—particularly on the way back from the funeral.

His chief gamekeeper, however, who also held the office of general manager in Zinkeneck, considered this an excellent opportunity to ask him a few questions. The gamekeeper was a fine, upstanding man. But, like all fine, upstanding employees, he was regularly being left in the lurch by his employer. For one thing, he scarcely ever got a chance to speak to Jessiersky, and when he did, he found it impossible to get any clear instructions out of him.

"Use your own judgment," would be Jessiersky's nonchalant

reply to most of his questions. But later on, for no discernible reason, he would fly into a rage and tell the man that he could not have acted more stupidly.

While Jessiersky walked on ahead with the chief gamekeeper, the relatives followed behind, talking to the children and wondering how long they themselves could possibly prolong their stay in Zinkeneck as mourners—the present occasion being probably the last one for capitalizing on their relationship with the deceased. The gamekeeper, meanwhile, was talking as hard as he could to Jessiersky. What particularly was on his mind this time was the situation in the neighboring preserve.

"All I ask of you," said Jessiersky, "is to tend to our own preserve."

Certainly, agreed the gamekeeper, he was doing that. But that was just why the situation in the adjoining place worried him so much. The hunting grounds there belonged to a Baron Koller who, being hard up for money, leased out shooting rights left and right, and, in fact, shooting rights for more game than there was.

"If it were not a case of a baron in need of money," Jessiersky said, "I would call it a swindle."

Yes, said the gamekeeper, that it was. But the worst of it was that Baron Koller's men, in order not to lose the "trophy money," had begun to bring their hunting guests over to the Zinkeneck property. And the guests either didn't notice or simply went along without bothering to protest.

"What nerve!" exclaimed Jessiersky, who, in reality, cared no more for his own chamois than for Koller's.

Actually, the gamekeeper told him, the Koller preserve itself had been kept going for some time only on the game that moved over from the Zinkeneck preserve.

"And it is quite wise for the game to do so," Jessiersky said, "for if it didn't change haunts, it would become too numerous and then we would have to shoot it ourselves. These things are regulated by Nature—it's only among humans that they are not regulated. When we have too many children, they cannot move over to another planet, with the result that before long we're all going to be annihilated down here."

The gamekeeper, who, like all simple people, was convinced that the world could never fall into such a state of disorder as the educated people believed, did not understand this remark. So he merely said, "But if the game move back again, the Koller game-keepers and their guests will simply come after them, and their excuse will be that in the high mountains it is impossible to tell exactly where boundaries are."

"Well, yes," said Jessiersky in bored tones, "but you can't tie up either the game or the men."

The gamekeeper glanced at him out of the corner of his eye and then asked him for authorization to take action against the Koller people.

"Don't kill anyone, for goodness' sake!" exclaimed Jessiersky. "In the city no one pays very much attention when a man is murdered. But out here all hell breaks loose."

The gamekeeper replied that he had no intention of having the trespassers shot on sight—though his men and he, too, had wished often enough to put a bullet into those fellows over there! There was one guest in particular who, as he and his men had learned, had purchased the right to shoot no less than four cham-ois bucks—a man by the name of Count Luna who, disregarding all protests, had several times …

"What?" cried Jessiersky.

"… come far in over the boundary," completed the gamekeeper. Jessiersky came to an abrupt halt.

The gamekeeper, pleased at Jessiersky's unexpected interest, stopped also, and the mourners behind them stood still and gazed in astonishment at the two men whose sudden stop made the chamois brushes on their hats shake as though with excitement.

"What did you say?" cried Jessiersky again. "*What* is the name of this man who …"

"A Count Luna, or whatever way you pronounce it," replied the gamekeeper who had become slightly unsure of himself.

Jessiersky remained silent for a moment. "I am going crazy," he thought. "So the fellow came here after all; he followed me even here! I deluded myself when I thought he wouldn't dare to!" But where had Luna got the money to pay for four chamois? "What does he look like?" Jessiersky asked excitedly. "Have you seen him?"

"Only through the field glasses."

"Well? And what does he look like? I want to know!"

Alas, the gamekeeper said, he was a very good-looking gentleman. He meant to imply that it was most regrettable that such an aristocratic person should let himself be taken into a preserve he had no right to enter, probably guided, because of his rank, by two of Baron Koller's men.

"By two?"

Yes.

Jessiersky stared at him. "And what does he *really* look like?" he asked again. "Is he thin or fat?"

Fairly thin.

"Does he have smallpox scars on his face?"

"Does he what?"

"Is he pockmarked?"

That he didn't know, said the gamekeeper. As he had mentioned before, he had seen him only through the binoculars and from quite a distance.

"Where does he live?" Jessiersky inquired. "In Schreinbach?"

No, replied the gamekeeper, unfortunately not. He himself had gone to look him up there and ask him not to let himself be led into the neighboring preserve because he might get treated to a load of fine shot like any common poacher. But in Schreinbach, he learned that the count did not live there. One of the Koller men, who were all rogues—getting friendly with people and then poaching on their preserves—had told him in the inn at Schreinbach, where he had stopped for a beer after his fruitless excursion, that the count had never had any intention of staying there. Immediately upon his arrival, he had gone to the preserve and had been spending his nights in one hunting shack after another. Never once had he come down to the valley, because "you have to really apply yourself" if you were going to get four chamois bucks when they were not there, at least not in the Koller preserve—as the fellow had had the nerve to add.

Jessiersky listened to this tale, or rather, he was not really listening. He seemed to be staring, past his employee, into space. Then he suddenly left the gamekeeper and the mourners and started back at a rapid pace, almost on the run, for the castle. He did not appear for dinner, which was served soon afterward to his guests, but could be heard rummaging about in his rooms and in the hall where the two gun cases stood. What he was looking for, as he angrily informed the servant he had called away from his duties at table, was a particular kind of cartridge containing bullets without a steel jacket. They were used for target shooting with Mannlicher rifles. He pulled open the drawers of both gun cases, but found nothing and immediately discharged two of the servants whom he blamed for the disappearance of the cartridges. Finally he began searching through the guest rooms and at long last discovered the cartridges in the chest of drawers in the bedroom of his father-in-law.

Old Pilas had not gone down to dinner. He had remained in his room to be alone with his grief. "Do you mean to say that you'll be going target shooting *today*?" the old man cried out indignantly.

"Be quiet, please!" shouted Jessiersky, put the cartridges in a knapsack, and sent a manservant to the kitchen with the order to pack up enough food for a few days.

Meanwhile the other mourners had finished their meal. They appeared in the corridor on the upper floor and through the open door watched Jessiersky rummaging about in old Pilas' room. Was he actually leaving, they inquired uneasily, and if so, would he allow them to stay on for a while longer in his absence?

"Stay if you want or go to hell for all of me!" he replied irritably and ran down the stairs, the knapsack in his hand. The next day he vanished from the house at the crack of dawn.

By no stretch of the imagination could Alexander Jessiersky be said to have any great enthusiasm for hunting. He hated having to leave the house at a ridiculous hour in the morning to go after a cock with a lantern or, if the quarry was merely a roebuck, to have his already freezing knees lashed by damp grass for hours. He abhorred shirts wringing with perspiration, heavy knapsacks, hobnail shoes, and loden capes with their offensive smell. He could think of far pleasanter pastimes than sliding about on slippery paths or breaking his knuckles in the talus. Every now and then he could be persuaded to go out deerstalking early in the evening, but any other shooting that had to be done he left to his gamekeepers or to occasional guests. But he had no great fondness for these either; they regularly repaid his hospitality by disturbing him at table with their foolish chatter. So he issued fewer and fewer invitations. The result of all this was that the neighboring preserves were kept going almost entirely by the game which went on and on reproducing itself over his land and sometimes moved over the boundary in whole herds.

It was his specialty, on the other hand, to take walks in the valley, scanning the peaks through a pair of strong binoculars to observe the activity of the game. Not unlike people who are so experienced in reading maps that even the barest sketch is full of meaning for them, he "read," not so much out of interest, perhaps, as out of boredom, a great deal of what went on up in the mountains. In the course of time, he began to notice more and more things which a less experienced observer would have overlooked. His gamekeeper, who at first had been baffled by his knowledge, had long since concluded that Jessiersky had not actually stayed down in the valley all the time, but from time to time, behind their backs, had gone up into the mountains.

This time he did go up. He ordered a carriage drawn by the two palominos to be brought at early dawn to take him as far as possible up the Gihon valley.

Just as he was leaving, the chief gamekeeper, having got wind of his plan, appeared in a nightshirt smelling of old sweat and took the liberty of inquiring where Herr Jessiersky was going.

To a place, replied Jessiersky, holding his nose, where he himself could put a stop to the activities of these gentlemen who were coming over from the neighboring preserve to hunt on his property.

Hadn't he perhaps better leave that to him and his men, by giving them permission to shoot, the gamekeeper inquired anxiously.

No, said Jessiersky, that he did not want to do, and anyway, he was never going to leave anything to anybody again, for he had seen what happened when he did.

Thereupon, the gamekeeper, in a piqued tone, asked whether he did not want to take at least one of the men along with him.

That, replied Jessiersky, he did not want to do either. He couldn't stand having people trail after him all the time. Under no conditions must the gamekeeper and his men come after him secretly! And, instead of asking questions here, he had now better hold back the dogs so that *they* wouldn't run after the carriage.

With this Jessiersky slung the binoculars over his shoulder and climbed into the carriage in which gun, knapsack, and loden cape had already been stowed. A lap robe was spread over his knees. The horses began to pull and, with white manes and tails fluttering in the breeze, bore him out of sight of the deeply offended chief gamekeeper.

Chapter 9

Jessiersky rode up the valley of the Gihon, which was really the Schrein Brook, or Schreinbach, from which the village below Zinkeneck had taken its name. As they went on, the road became scarcely distinguishable from the brook bed beside which it ran; and finally the horses, though pulling with all their might, could not budge the carriage another inch uphill. Jessiersky got out, loaded the knapsack on his back, and had the driver pull the loden cape through the straps. He picked up his gun and, to be on the safe side, removed its cap and put it into his pocket. Then he took a last look at the carriage and the sweat-drenched palominos which were recovering their wind; and as the driver lowered the whip in his farewell salute, Jessiersky shouldered his walking stick, turned about, and began to ascend the slope of the Hochzinken.

His path led him first through sparse woods where the tall grass, interspersed with clumps and clusters of gentians, came up above his knees, then over upland pastures. All around him the Alps unfolded like an ocean of petrified waves that had been lashed up by some monstrous storm. Toward noon he reached the region of the gorges through which ran the boundary between his preserve and Koller's.

Here the sun was beating down with all its force on the rocky peaks which rose up in a long row into the dark blue sky. The brilliance of the rocks dazzled and blurred Jessiersky's vision: it was as though black shadows were passing by. A kind of luminous shower seemed to be pouring down from a storm of light, and if a real storm had gathered, its shadows would scarcely have been distinguishable from the darkness of the sky, its billowing white cloud towers from the bone-white towers of the cliffs. It was all as still as eternity. Only the grass, dotted with the spring flowers of the upland summer, with mountain cornflowers, forget-me-nots, and primroses, whispered in the sunny wind; and away in the distance, almost as if from nowhere, the tinkle of sheep bells could be heard. But no animal was in sight. A hut nearby—a kind of stable made of rough stones—which must have been built as a shelter for the sheep, lay in ruins, and the rotten wood of the caved-in roof gave off an odor in the noonday heat. Perhaps the herds were grazing along the margins of two or three pools or lakes of transparent emerald that had formed at the foot of the peaks in the titanic maze of moss-covered boulders.

To Jessiersky it seemed ludicrous that this awe-inspiring landscape should be registered in his name, but still more so that it should once have been owned by old Fries. Here, then, in this all but lunar landscape he would put a stop to the activities of the moon! Indeed, the scenery here resembled certain areas of the moon's surface even more closely than did the land around the city of Luna on the map. Was it six months now or longer that he had been poring over that map in his library when for the first time he had heard Luna's footsteps passing high above his head—although probably it had not been Luna at all?

He threw down his pack and took shelter in the shade of the ruined hut. Surrounded with stinging nettles, which were growing rampant here, and a swarm of flies which refused to be beaten off, he took up his binoculars and carefully surveyed the landscape before him. He now discovered the sheep which were standing on strips of grass on the mountainside above the lakes. He also saw all sorts of game which, perhaps because of the heat, were moving very slowly, but nowhere did he discern any human being. Finally he got to his feet, picked up his goods and chattels, and walked for about an hour and a half down over the steep slope until he came to inhabited pastures. One of them, on which there were three herdsmen's huts, he decided to make his headquarters.

Whereas the path over which he had just come had been very steep, the ground from here on sloped down rather more gently into the valley. But here too the rays of the noonday sun were beating down with merciless force. It was not only the sun, however, which had made its power felt here. Fire had also raged pitilessly, for the tops of most of the firs that were growing here and there along the slope had been seared by lightning. The cruel ravages of water were also evident. Probably during the same storms that had decapitated the trees, the meadowland had been ripped up to its yellow-brown depths by raging torrents, and in places there were piles of talus as high as a man which had been washed down from the peaks.

The hut standing highest on the slope being the first to which he came, Jessiersky walked in. He threw down his load and seated himself wearily beside the hearth. Except for his brief stop by the gorges, he had been under way since early morning. He took off his shoes. It was hot and musty in the hut, and in the adjacent stall, the cattle were pacing about and banging against the walls. From the room above under the roof, where the hay was stored, came a voice asking who was there. Jessiersky irritably called out to whomever it was to be silent, adding that if anyone wanted to know who was there he could come and see for himself. Whereupon a half-grown boy came sliding down from the hay loft. Recognizing Jessiersky, he greeted him and began at once to gather up the scattered possessions.

Jessiersky, meanwhile, remained seated by the hearth, stretching his aching legs and examining the blisters that had formed on his feet. Finally he stood up, walked to the door, sat down again on the threshold, and lighted a cigarette.

A kind of porch had been constructed here. The floor consisted of some planks which were raised up horizontally above the slanting ground of the pasture, and the roof, an extension of the hut roof, was supported by two wooden uprights. Not far away, by the fence, which enclosed a pile of cattle fodder, the so-called swath, a little stream of water was trickling out of a pipe into a wooden trough, and the mud all around it had been trampled by the hoofs of cattle. Nothing could be heard but the spring and nothing was stirring here or in either of the other two huts. Poor and miserable as they were, they seemed to have been built solidly and well. How many generations of mountain herdsmen they must have sheltered from rainstorms and the noonday heat! And the breath of the glaciers seemed to be still present in the wind that was blowing against the slope. They rose up in the distance, behind the rigid stony desert of the lesser peaks, now bathed in cataracts of light, now illumined by flickering sunbeams, now lost in billowing clouds, now swathed in smoky shadows.

Meanwhile, a young woman, who must have been in her room sleeping—for mountain herders do most of their work at night—came out of the hut. She came up behind Jessiersky, walking noiselessly on her bare feet, and greeted him. He turned about and glanced up at her fleetingly. Then, his eyes fixed once again on the distant glaciers, he announced that he would spend the night there. "And, by the way, bring me my field glass," he added.

While she was getting the binoculars, he saw the boy, who must have left the hut by the stall door, run down over the pasture to the two other huts. From there he returned with two or three other young people and one elderly woman. They went into the hut, again through the stable door, and Jessiersky heard them behind him whispering with one another.

He had focused the binoculars first upon the ice fields, which at one moment were dazzlingly brilliant and the next a dull gray, then upon the misty stone ridges of the peaks, and finally upon the ancient fir trees farther off in the pasture. They were the last outposts of a forest that stretched from the foot of the pastureland down into a dark, ravine-like valley and its roaring stream. How old those trees really were it was impossible to say, but they must have been there for several centuries. Their roots coiled in and out of the ground around them like clusters of enormous snakes. Their branches were enveloped in moss and lichen, and their spiked tops reached up toward the sky like the points of lances. The stiff skeletons of some of the dead trees were still standing like gigantic whisk brooms, and one was completely hollow. It had an opening like a sentinel box, and the wood seemed thinner than a wasp's nest, so that a person could poke holes in it with his bare fingers. Others, broken up into gray pieces, were lying in a maze of dead branches, resembling blackened whale ribs. The entire pile was resting on a bed of mountain fescue and hawk-weed, mild vetch and lady's-mantle, yarrow and spignet. Others, although reduced to shapeless fragments, were still surrounded with clouds of dark green needles. There was not a tree that, at its base, could be encircled by fewer than three men, not a trunk that did not divide into several trunks, not a cluster of trunks that had not branched out, like a huge chandelier, into enormous perpendicular arms. There was not one of these firs and pines that was not in itself a whole forest, some parts of it living, some rotting, some dead; deciduous trees had taken root and animals of all kinds sheltered in its glades and impenetrable thickets. The timber of any one of these trees would have sufficed to build a sizable boat.

As Jessiersky looked at the trees, one after the other, he began once more to ponder the question of their age. There were other trees elsewhere that were undoubtedly far older than these; the oaks in Germany, for example, a few of which may even go back to the days of the pagans; the araucaria in Mexico on the "Hill of Locusts," the site of the summer residence of the hapless Montezuma and of the no less hapless Maximilian; or even the tremendous sequoias in California. But what made the firs here older than all other trees was the fact that their age was unremembered. In other words, even if their age could be recalled, no one had ever recalled it. It was impossible that one of the peasants who owned one of the three huts might have heard from his father's father that one of these trees had been comparatively young when that grandfather was a boy. For the trees were not in actual fact so terribly old. But neither the grandfather nor the grandson spoke about the age of these trees, nor had they ever spoken about it, and this made the trees timelessly old. There were other timeless things here. In fact, from this point of view, everything was timeless.

Down at the edge of the forest, for instance, were the remains of a fodder shed on which Jessiersky kept close watch, imagining that Luna might have stationed himself there to keep an eye on the huts. And because of his long experience in using the binoculars, he could tell that the wood the shed was built of had been used before for other purposes. In several of the planks there were notches where other planks had been joined to them. But the other boards were not there and perhaps no longer existed. They may once have been part of the roof of a hut that had also long ceased to exist.

There might be people who knew or might have known at what period the shed was built. It might have been put up during the time of Napoleon. And the hut, whose roof had been used in its construction, might, perhaps, have been another hundred or hundred and fifty years older. But nothing around here could go back more than four hundred and fifty years. For it was then that Emperor Maximilian I had first settled the region with his huntsmen. The peasants either were descended from these huntsmen or had migrated here later on. Before that time, there had been nothing but wilderness.

But no one gave a thought to the emperor, his hunters, his own ancestors, or the number of years that had passed. If something here was old, it could be a hundred or a thousand years old, or even much older. It made no difference, for it had dropped out of time, or might even have passed far beyond it. In such surroundings it seemed a little petty, almost ridiculous, to take too seriously the things that were still within time, the events still taking place—such as this conflict with Luna! But Luna himself, if he were really named after the moon, which was certainly very old, should have behaved a great deal more timelessly. He ought not to have purchased shooting rights in the next preserve in order to come over here to shoot someone down....

Jessiersky was still looking through the field glass when the young woman from the hut came up behind him again and offered him her room for the night. She herself, she said, obviously following the advice of her neighbors, would go up to the hay loft.

Jessiersky laid down the binoculars for a moment, thanked her with a faint smile, and told her to go right on sleeping in her room. He himself, he said, would either sleep in the hay or not sleep at all. He then took up the field glass again.

Toward evening, without his knapsack and loden cape, but

equipped with the Mannlicher, the ammunition, and the field glass, Jessiersky was back once again in the region of the gorges.

This time he discovered, far away on the other side of the boundary line, two people who were obviously stalking game and behaving in a manner characteristic of gamekeeper and sportsman guest. There was no doubt, therefore, that it was one of Koller's men with a guest of Koller. The gamekeeper walked ahead and did the scouting. The guest, who followed behind, did no scouting at all, leaving that task to the gamekeeper. As a result he would be totally unprepared should the gamekeeper suddenly push him into the trees and ask him to shoot at a chamois that had already taken off like a bolt of lightning. However, there was little danger of that in the Koller grounds; there were hardly any chamois left there. As Jessiersky saw only two people, he decided that it could not be Luna—who, as his own gamekeeper had said, was accompanied regularly by *two* Koller men! Jessiersky, therefore, carefully searched the Koller preserve still further and studied in particular the pastures where the cattle had been let out after having been kept in the huts all day. He saw several herd boys and milkmaids but no sportsmen. He did find at least one of the Koller hunting huts, but nothing was stirring anywhere around it.

Night was falling as he walked back. There were flashes of rose-colored sheet lightning above the far-off glaciers.

That night there was a heavy storm, and the herders were out searching until early morning for a few head of cattle that had lost their way in the downpour.

It continued to rain for two full days. Jessiersky, who remained in the hut—with the poor visibility it would have been futile to leave it—made advances to the milkmaid, partly out of boredom, partly out of nervousness. And as the pasturelands were enclaves in the Zinkeneck property, the young woman did not dare rebuff him; he could have made it very unpleasant for both her and the peasant she worked for. It was indeed singular, now that Luna was closer than ever to him, that he should make advances to this woman, when before, obsessed by the thought of Luna, he had so neglected his wife that Spinette had finally had to pay with his life for it. But such things always operate according to the laws of singularity rather than those of reason. And in the end it was to turn out that to behave in this singular fashion was the wisest thing Jessiersky could have done.

On the morning of the third day, the rain stopped and Jessiersky betook himself once again to the gorges where he saw a large number of animals but no human being. On the way back, however, on a slope far below him, he caught sight of his gamekeeper who, apparently worried by his long absence, had come to look for him. Jessiersky, although far from a perfect shot, picked up his gun with the telescopic sight and, for a joke, planted a shell in the gravel right at the gamekeeper's feet. The lead shot exploded on the stones, and the gamekeeper, more deeply offended than ever, vanished in the direction of the valley.

But on the evening of that day, Jessiersky discovered a group of three people approaching from the Koller preserve. He sat down once again beside the ruined hut, and hiding behind a clump of nettles, watched the movements of the men, the binoculars shaking in his trembling hands.

The men were carrying guns, and their walking sticks moved as rhythmically as lances. Two of them, the gamekeepers apparently, were walking about one hundred steps ahead, and the third, probably Luna, was following. But this was not the proper way to stalk game. The two men in front would certainly startle the game prematurely and the guest would have no chance to shoot! This was a kind of battle march, and Luna was using the two men to protect himself from being shot at unexpectedly in the alien preserve. And unless this march, which had already been attempted several times before, were halted, it would continue on to Zinkeneck, into the castle, to Jessiersky himself....

When the group had crossed the boundary and had advanced almost a thousand feet beyond it, Jessiersky could see the men clearly and he was sure that he recognized Luna. He had never really seen him, but how could that slender body and that head, which was a little too large, that haughty carriage, and the pushed-in face with the pockmarks belong to anybody else? Jessiersky stared through the field glass without once averting his eyes, as though simply by staring at him he could compel the elusive adversary to come to him. When they were within six hundred feet of him, he let the binoculars, on their straps, drop onto his chest and felt for the gun. His eyes still riveted on the approaching group, he raised the gun to his cheek and tried to watch Luna through the telescopic sight. But his hands were trembling like those of a real sportsman when he is suddenly confronted with a royal stag. At five hundred feet, he raised the gun again, put his finger to the trigger, and tried to aim. It would have been wise to have waited a little longer before shooting. The group was approaching slowly and steadily over fairly level pastureland. But he simply did not have the nerve to wait. It seemed to him that if he did not shoot now, he might never be able to shoot—that, in fact, it might be too late already! But as he tried nevertheless to cover Luna's breast with the intersection of the cross hairs, it occurred to him that he had not set the sight for the proper distance. He therefore lowered the gun and examined it. The sight, after his shot at the feet of the gamekeeper, was still set at five hundred. He raised the rifle again, but with a feeling of futility, as though he were trying to bring down a bird on the wing with a stone, or to strangle a ghost with his bare hands. Everything became blurred, and he could see virtually nothing. But after a few seconds he pulled the trigger, felt the back kick of the telescopic sight against his eye sockets, and heard the shrill whine of the bullet.

Curiously enough, his nervousness vanished in a flash, and he was able to watch the shot through the telescopic sight. He saw that it was not Luna who was knocked down by the shot, but one of the two men ahead of him. Luna and the other man had immediately flung themselves on the ground and crawled behind the jagged rocks that were scattered over the pasture. Jessiersky at once fired the rest of the magazine at the spot where Luna was lying, and at the third or fourth shot he saw the dust fly high in the air.

But now Luna and the other sportsman, although they could not see Jessiersky, and only knew the general direction from which he had been shooting, were firing back. Jessiersky, hearing the shots whine past him and ricochet from the stone wall of the hut, threw himself down into the nettles, raised the Mannlicher, and discharged a second and third magazine against the rocks behind which Luna was hiding.

Meanwhile, the fallen sportsman was lying motionless in full view. The shots fired by Luna and the other man soon became more infrequent. The two men apparently had only a few more shells. The echo was tossed back and forth across the gorge and gradually died away. Before long their shooting stopped altogether.

Jessiersky, however, kept on firing until nightfall, at the place where he supposed Luna to be. He used up virtually the entire supply of ammunition with which he had stuffed his pockets several days before—nearly seventy shells in all.

Then he heard Luna and his man call each other in the darkness. He concluded that they had decided to get up, and a little later he, in fact, heard them running off across the pasture, pounding like deer. He too got up, walked over to the place where they had been lying, and examined the ground by the light of some matches. The man he had hit with the first shot had undoubtedly been killed instantly. The shot had ripped open the top of his skull; had Jessiersky's wavering gun moved so much as a hair's breadth to the left or right, the shot would have dropped into empty space. But where Luna and the other fellow had been lying, he found only empty shells—no blood, no sign that either had been hurt. Even with more than five dozen shots, Jessiersky had been unable to hit his adversary. On the field of battle, so he had heard, it was as a rule necessary to fire off a man's weight in ammunition to kill him; to finish off Luna, it would perhaps have required a quantity of ammunition equal to the weight of the moon.

Chapter 10

"Why," Jessiersky asked himself as he stumbled back over the pasture, toward the ruined hut, "was I so set on using duck shot? Was it because lead sits like butter in the rifling and is supposed to be a fraction of a degree more accurate than steel? But when you aim at one enemy and hit another, you might just as well have used steel. Or did I insist on using lead bullets because they would lose their shape and no one would be able to tell who shot what at whom, and what kind of rifle he used? True, if only two or three bullets are shot off, they usually flatten out, and often the majority will spatter onto the stones and become unrecognizable; but out of sixty or seventy shots at least a dozen will remain intact, and anyone can tell in a moment they came from a Mannlicher, caliber such and such. Exactly because they are made of lead, it will be all the easier to find out who was misguided enough to use them!"

But at the same time he felt somewhat relieved, if only because he no longer had to carry around the ammunition which had been weighing him down for the past few days. How far off could the noise of the shooting have been heard, he wondered, and when would they come to gather up the dead and wounded of the battle. For it must have sounded like a regular battle! "Probably they won't come for a long time, or maybe not at all. They will pretend not to know—those people are always anxious not to get involved."

Meanwhile, he had groped his way back to the ruin and began

to look for the empty shells. He got his fingers stung by nettles in the search and used up all of his matches. "What am I doing?" he wondered. "I can never find all the shells. They have rolled in among the nettles or into the talus. But even if I found all of them, what good would it do me? What with the sensation I have caused by choosing to come up here for the first time in so many years, the excitement of my chief gamekeeper and the wide-eyed amazement of the household, the police are bound to arrest me, whether they find the empty shells or not!"

But unlucky as he had been in his attempt to shoot Luna, he was to be very lucky indeed when the case came to be investigated. In the first place, that same night, all telltale prints of hobnail shoes, of elbows which might have been pressed into the ground by a man leveling his gun, and any scent that police dogs might have followed—all such clues were completely washed away by a fresh downpour. In the second place, it did not occur to anyone that Jessiersky could possibly have shot the man, a certain Eisl, the father of five minor children. As Jessiersky's chief gamekeeper had been foolish enough to disobey the express orders of his employer and had followed him into the critical area, the police assumed that it was he who had fired at Eisl. He was immediately jailed and held for a time during which it was proved that he shot the same caliber gun as his employer and, at least on the rifle range, used duck shot as well. It also became quite clear why Jessiersky had forbidden the gamekeeper to follow him. For the woman he had spent the night with very shortly announced that she was expecting a child by him. There could be no doubt, therefore, that he had gone up to the mountain pastures for this purpose, although it had been perhaps a trifle too soon after his wife's death, and not in order to commit a murder.

If the stupid and primitive notions, so typical of the country and the people, had worked against him instead of to his advantage, it would have thrown Jessiersky into a frenzy. As it was, he felt as if he really were becoming insane only when it was brought home to him not only that he had killed Eisl to no purpose, but that—as was revealed in the course of the investigation—this particular Luna was not Luna at all. That is to say, the man's name *was* Luna, but he was by no means the obscure would-be university lecturer who was Jessiersky's mortal enemy. He was a real Luna, of the family of Azlor de Aragon which appears in every court almanac—where, in fact, Jessiersky had found it. It was just like his gamekeeper, a man of fine character but limited intelligence, to have considered it superfluous to inform Jessiersky that the gentleman who had purchased shooting rights in the Koller preserve was a Spaniard!

Incidentally, the gentleman was conspicuous not only by reason of his foreign origin, but also on account of his stinginess. In his own country, where he had shot the native varieties of the ibex, the *Capra pyrenaica* in the Pyrenees and the *Capra hispanica* in the Sierra Nevada, he had become consumed with the desire to bag some Alpine ibexes as well. Upon learning that this was a costly project both in Switzerland and in Italy—where a high fee is demanded for the shooting of ibexes—he had a Prince Porcia, who acted as agent, buy for him the right to shoot four chamois bucks in the Koller preserve. But, as one of the Koller gamekeepers had so correctly observed in the Schreinbach inn, it turned out that there simply were not four chamois left in that preserve. And the Spaniard, instead of accepting the fact that he had been cheated, insisted on getting his money's worth. He began trespassing upon the neighboring preserve—which was why he always had *two* men walk ahead of him! The Koller men, who had long before ceased to pay much attention to boundaries, were not themselves averse to his poaching. If the Spaniard, then, had been reasonably prudent, the two gamekeepers of Baron Koller certainly had not—as was proved by the firing duel with Jessiersky.

At any rate, the Spaniard was required to pay a high fine, and he left the country cursing, without so much as a single chamois horn as a trophy.

Jessiersky, anxious to find out exactly which Luna he was, sent to Vienna for the court almanac and looked through it. This Luna, he decided, must have been Ferdinand, Count and Duke of Luna, born March 2, 1910, at San Sebastian, the eldest son of José Antonio (17th Duke of Villahermosa, 6th Duke of Granada de Ega, Lord Marshal of Navarre, twice Grandee of Spain, 1st class, former Lord Chamberlain of the Prince and Princess of Asturia, Knight of the Sovereign Order of the Knights of Malta) and his wife, née Isabel de Guillamas Caro Pineyro y Széchenyi.

In spite of all that, however, Jessiersky could not rid himself of the idea that the person really behind this entire episode had been another Ferdinand Luna, the sociologist and one-time prisoner in the Ebensee concentration camp.

This may explain why, after attending the hearing in Vienna on his collision with the two motorcyclists, he returned once again to Zinkeneck, and also why he did not send the children back to school. Instead, they were given, in addition to Mademoiselle, a private tutor. This man, although he appeared to be rather bored with the solitude of the countryside, for some reason discharged his duty most conscientiously.

It was the time of year when the summer hangs over into the fall, and this particular year it hung on far longer than usual, as though it saw no reason for coming to an end. One day was very much like another, and they were all very much like summer days. But in a way this Indian summer was not summertime any more. Everywhere insects of a kind not commonly found in these parts kept appearing. They swarmed about, flitted in the fading light of the season, and finally found their way into the house. Even long after the autumn rains had begun and it was almost time for snow, they could be found behind the window shutters and picture frames, in the unoccupied rooms, under the chests in the hall, in the attic, and in other remote corners of the house, from which they would emerge again around All Saints' Day, or whenever there were a few mild days. Even in spring their fragile corpses could still be found clinging to the deserted, dusty spider webs. There were some years, and these were in the majority, when these strange varieties of gnats, flies, and butterflies did not get a chance to exist; actually they were always ready to come into being. Every August, particularly, they were, so to speak, on the threshold of existence; but then so many bad Septembers came along, they were almost never able to achieve it. For years they would lie in wait for the opportunity to come into being, confident that the year was bound to come that would give them life. At last such a year would come, and they existed. But then, it was as though their existence already belonged to the past, so strangely, so much like ghosts, did they stagger through time.

Sometimes, when Jessiersky was lying on the lawn by a cluster of hazels and watching one of these swarms of gnats playing in the sun—or when walking along one of the bridle paths around Zinkeneck toward evening, he would stop to gaze at the tiny, transparent butterflies whirling about in the weak sunlight— he could not help feeling that his own life, not unlike the life of these insects, had stretched on into a time in which, even to him, it seemed a life no longer his, a life stained with crimes not his, which should long since have come to an end. He remembered that once, in his boyish vanity, he had wished to be more like his ancestors, and to display the ugliest characteristics, if only they were his forebears'. Now he *was* very much like them, had probably even surpassed them; not one of them would have had to be ashamed of the horrible traits their descendant exhibited. But he had not at all wanted to do what he had done, and it seemed to him that it was not *he* who had done these things, but one of them! But had not that very fact made him one of them? Was he really still himself?

In November the investigation of Eisl's shooting was closed, although no conclusion had been reached. Since it had been impossible to establish the guilt of Jessiersky's chief gamekeeper, he was let out of jail. The police had unearthed from the battlefield a few lead bullets of the caliber he used that were practically intact, but these were not, in themselves, final proof of his guilt. It was clear that the person, or persons, who had waged this battle with the Spaniard and the two Koller men must have belonged to the Zinkeneck estate. For if they had been poachers, even if there had been three or four of them, they would never have opened fire, but would simply have retreated. Still the identity of the Zinkeneck men who supposedly had shot Eisl remained undiscovered. As mentioned previously, it had occurred to no one—or, at least, to hardly anyone—that it might have been Jessiersky, after all. While at the outset, it *had* seemed strange that a few days prior to Eisl's shooting he had been searching the house for shells containing the kind of lead shot with which Eisl was killed, this damaging evidence was not taken seriously, so little did anyone believe a man like Jessiersky capable of any extraordinary action, whether criminal or otherwise. For in the country, and particularly among the rural bureaucracy, people would believe anything—as became abundantly evident in the course of the investigation—except that a rich man like Jessiersky would be moved to do something that only poor people, such as his gamekeepers, were expected to do. In short, the regard for his person, which in theory was so high and in practice so low, would certainly have annoyed Jessiersky deeply had it not been for the fact that, failing to win the warrior's laurels in the upland, he had been crowned with the wild roses of rural romance. As for the lead shot he had been looking for in the house, the police assumed that he had wanted to give it to his chief gamekeeper: and this—by local standards at least—he had a perfect right to do.

Meanwhile, however, the battle high in the mountains, which was supposed to have taken place simultaneously with his pastoral idyll, had become more and more popular throughout the region. Everyone talked not only about the battle, but also about those who had taken part in it, such as, for instance, the Count-Duke Luna, even though he had long since left the country. The word *count*—*Graf*—in those parts, is not only a title, but also the family name of a good many peasants. There are *Graf* peasants in many Austrian valleys, and Duke—*Herzog*—is a fairly common name, too. Having heard mention of a Count-Duke, the people, from the very outset, thought of him as someone they were familiar with, and, in the end, completely forgot that the man in question was a real count and duke in one person. Little by little the notion became implanted in their minds that he had been a rich peasant from the flat country who, instead of poaching as most peasants do, had been wealthy enough to purchase regular shooting rights; and upon discovering that he had been cheated, he then had actually begun to poach with the two Koller gamekeepers. And as the story spread, people grew quite willing to put the *Graf-Herzog* in a class with some of the ghostly wild huntsmen of their folklore.

At the time the chief gamekeeper was released from prison, the legend-building was in full swing. And the reputation that the investigation had earned him of having finished off one of the helpmates of the Great Huntsman clung to him fast. The gamekeeper himself cared little for that fame. He had sat in jail three and a half months and was the only person who knew he had sat there for Jessiersky. The good man had never once opened his mouth to betray his employer, nor did he ever betray him, although, when they met, Jessiersky hurt his feelings very much by remarking that another time he had better think twice before disobeying orders and spying on his employer. To him, Jessiersky began to become almost as sinister a figure as was the Count-Duke Luna to the people of the countryside—but not so sinister as the real Luna seemed to Jessiersky himself.

Jessiersky had no idea where Luna had been during the time all this had been happening. But he was convinced, although he tried to persuade himself of the absurdity of the notion, that Luna must be staying somewhere nearby—this is evident from the following:

There was first of all the fact that this winter in Zinkeneck was unusually mild, and in the amount of frost and snow, in the frequency and severity of storms, differed perceptibly from the weather prevailing in Schreinbach or in regions a little further away. The severity of a winter in a given place depends above all on its latitude and upon its height above sea level. In general, the higher a place is in the Northern Hemisphere, the lower it is in the Southern Hemisphere—and the higher it is above the sea—the colder the winter will be. The sea level of a given place does not change, but conditions in a given latitude, which in itself remains constant, are, nevertheless, over long periods of time, subject to variations which are the result of a changing relation to the position of the sun. Ages ago in Zinkeneck, for example, the sun certainly rose higher or less high above the horizon than it does today, and in the future, too, there will be variations. For the angle formed by the earth's axis, or the equator, with the apparent orbit of the sun, or the actual orbit of the earth, is constantly changing, and the declination of the earth's axis is also subject to change, though that change is very slow. Sometimes, in the course of millenniums, it rises; at other times, over an equally long period of time, it dips. As a result, the winters gradually become either more severe with more snow, or milder; and the summers gradually grow warmer and more rainy, or cooler. Thus at present, the obliquity of the sun's orbit, or ecliptic, is decreasing at the rate of .4758 seconds per year, and after the passage of millenniums, it will have decreased to 21 degrees and then will slowly increase again. The limits within which it varies are from 6 to 7 degrees apart. According to the investigations of these periods made by Lagrange, the obliquity of the ecliptic was greatest in the year 29,400 B.C., that is, 27 degrees and 31 minutes. For fifteen thousand years after that time, it decreased and reached its smallest value, 21 degrees and 20 minutes, in the year 14,400 B.C. Since then, it has been increasing and reached its maximum value, 23 degrees and 53 minutes, around 2000 B.C. The ecliptic has again been decreasing since then, and in the year 6600 A.D. will have again reached its smallest value of 22 degrees and 54 minutes—to grow once more, for another 12,700 years, until, in 19,300 A.D., it will have attained its greatest value of 25 degrees and 21 minutes.

What had originally brought about this variability of the obliquity of the ecliptic, which in its turn determined the character of winters and summers, and was probably also responsible for the glacial periods, Heaven only knew. Jessiersky certainly did not know and he did not care. But the moon, along with a number of other forces, undoubtedly also influenced the ecliptic and the variability of the seasons—and this fact interested Jessiersky very much indeed. For the magnetic power of the moon, like a kitten playing with the knitting needles stuck in a ball of wool, tugged at the earth's axis and pulled it out of line.

Had he simply told himself that if, after a few thousand years, the winters were to become milder than at present, this would be due in part to the moon, such a thought would have been well within the realm of science. But the notion that the mildness of this particular winter, which was felt only, or mainly, in Zinkeneck, and may have been noticeable only to him, was due to a lunar influence, that is, to Luna—this was more than an aberration; it bordered on insanity.

At least Jessiersky did not as yet think that Luna was the moon itself. Apparently he believed merely that Luna had been endowed with much of the moon's powers, that he was a relative of the moon, a little moon, as it were. For if there had been sons of the sun, such as the Pharoahs and the Incas, why should there not be a grandson of the moon like this Luna? To be sure, his periods no longer coincided with those of the real moon, but they were of the same or almost the same duration. His attributes were decidedly lunar attributes. And if the real moon, by influencing the obliquity of the ecliptic, was able in the course of millenniums to make winters in the Northern Hemisphere milder, Luna no doubt was able to make this winter milder in Zinkeneck. This unusual mildness was proof positive of Luna's presence.... Jessiersky frequently toyed with these ideas, and when there were sudden thaws, when the south wind spread a filmy veil over the sky, or when warm, blue gray clouds from over the Hochzinken rolled into the valley, it was hard for him to dispel the notion that it was Luna who had evoked these phenomena....

Jessiersky occasionally talked to the children's tutor, Herr Achtner, a man of some education and an interesting fellow to converse with. Later, Jessiersky could not remember whether it was he or Achtner who had started those erudite conversations. It then would seem to him that it had been he. But it is more probable that it had been Achtner.

It was by now the end of April and the young woman Jessiersky had spent several nights with during the summer was about to give birth to the child which even before its birth had been its father's savior. One afternoon, Achtner went on a hike with his charges, to point out certain early spring flowers and to examine them with the children.

Jessiersky took advantage of this opportunity to do some examining of his own in Achtner's room. There he failed to find what he was looking for. But up in the attic, in one of Achtner's two suitcases, which were locked and which he broke open, he found what he had expected to find, the evidence that Achtner was a detective—his police badge and a service revolver. The latter he took.

"Inspector," he said, when Achtner returned, "I've always thought that the Austrian police revolver was too heavy to be carried comfortably in one's pocket. But to put it away in the attic until one needs it—which, as one thinks, won't be that soon—this is going a bit too far, isn't it? For then the person you wish to arrest can turn the tables. Be that as it may," he continued, while patting the right pocket of his trousers, "I thank you very much indeed for having tutored my children; you certainly were far more conscientious in that job than might have been expected from your carelessness in other respects. But now this period, which has been no less enjoyable for me and my family than for you, must come to an end, as must all other efforts you made here in Zinkeneck. And so you are now free to return home, Inspector."

Achtner turned pale and tried to talk his way out of the situation. "If you require me to go home now," he said, "you will spoil everything. It was my plan, before arresting you, to find evidence that it was you who murdered both Eisl and Spinette. Only then would I have arrested you, and if I hadn't been able to find evidence, I would simply have let you go free. But if you force me to leave before I have completed my assignment, you will disgrace me with my superiors and ruin my career—"

"Don't get sentimental, Inspector," Jessiersky interrupted. "Next thing you'll tell me you thought I really was a decent fellow who wouldn't break into ..."

"I had not, in fact, expected you to go in for burglary," Achtner said.

"Sure. If you had expected me to go in for it, you would not have left the revolver in the suitcase. You would have carried it with you. You should, in any case, have assumed me to be capable of forcing a suitcase and have kept the pistol constantly with you. For you know God is always on the side of the stronger battalions, don't you?" And again Jessiersky patted his pocket.

"God is always with the biggest rascals," said Achtner, "and if you really insist upon my leaving, I shall have to have you arrested."

"That's a good one!" laughed Jessiersky. "You can see for yourself where you've got without the spoils of my burglary! No, Herr Achtner, you will have to leave. What is more, you will leave at once. And to make quite sure that you do get on your way, I myself will take you to the station."

And this he did. About six o'clock in the evening, he climbed into the car with Achtner who had no choice but to obey. The children, upset by the sudden departure, bade their tutor a fond farewell, and the two men started off down the road which ran along the Pison.

But when Jessiersky reached the station, Achtner was not with him. He parked the car and boarded the train. And all through the night, as he rode toward Vienna, he had a distinct feeling that he was being pursued not by the police, but by Luna. The police, it was obvious, were fools. Only Luna could really bring about his downfall.

He remained in Vienna until the morning of the second of May, and set in order various things in his house and at the office. At noon on the second he left Vienna for Munich. On the fourth he went on to Milan and on the evening of the sixth arrived in Rome.

Chapter 11

Of all the hills of Rome, which, according to the ancients, are seven in number (although in more recent times the count has risen to eleven or twelve), the Capitoline is the smallest and most modest, but, historically, the most famous. Scarcely higher than a house, with a dip in the middle, it stands out among its fellows only because of its steep slopes and its position in the very heart of the city. In all probability it is no longer as high as it was originally, not because of the leveling that had to be done in order to provide building sites for the palaces and temples which adorn it, but because the ground surrounding it has risen; the dust and rubble of destruction, the wreckage of former grandeur, and the drifting sands of transiency have added to its height. Today, if anyone were to push a condemned criminal from the highest point of the Capitoline, the Tarpeian Rock, the man would get badly bumped and bruised, but it is most unlikely that he would die. Lowered, flattened, and overtaken by time, like Rome itself, even its most sacred peak is overshadowed by the pompous monument of the kings of the House of Savoy, which, in its turn, has been overtaken by time. Disturbed by the vulgar noise of the roaring traffic, eagles and she-wolves, symbols of a greater, higher, calmer power, sit mourning in their cages beneath the overhanging slopes of the hill.

That it was not the Campus Martius which was settled first, but the hills, the Capitoline and the Palatine—not low places such as the Velabrum and the Forum Boarium, but the elevations of

Rome, to name only the Cermalus and the Velia—is less in keeping with the tastes and the way of life of the Latin or Umbrian-Volscian inhabitants than with their heritage of Etruscan caution. But the Roman character, of course, is made up of a mixture of strains, Sabine, Etruscan and Latin, with a preponderance of Etruscan. Even the legend that the entire Roman patriciate is descended from the Trojans is Etruscan. The version according to which the national Latin god, Mars himself, and Rhea Sylvia, the daughter of Numitor of Alba and the granddaughter of Anchises, were the parents of Romulus and Remus is simply a laborious attempt to Italianize the legend.

The Etruscans, or as they called themselves, the Tyrrhenians, settled in Italy at the beginning of the first millennium before Christ, having migrated from the vicinity of Troy. They showed a marked tendency to make their home not on the sunburnt plains, but on the shady slopes of the valleys that had been carved by the rivers in the tufa tableland. On these steep, precipitous hills, they entrenched themselves behind strong fortifications, and here they passed their comfortable and lascivious lives. They feared death more than most peoples. Yet they, too, had to bow to fate.

Whoever has seen the remains of even a few Etruscan cities must realize that both the Capitoline and the Palatine were originally settled not by Latin but by Etruscan tribes. For these two hills—from which it was possible not only to prevent anyone from crossing the Tiber, but also to bar the way to ships approaching along the river—might well have reminded the Lydian immigrants of their native Thyrrha, or Tyrsa. Later on, these places fell into the hands of the Latins, but even today they are still haunted by the memory of their first inhabitants.

What strange, mysterious people! Their most striking characteristic seems to have been that they never tried to delude themselves about anything, however disagreeable, however tragic. Outwardly effeminate, yet incorruptible, these men and women took the span of life for exactly what it is; as an opportunity, never to return, to enjoy not, perhaps, the highest happiness, but the deepest, often the grossest pleasure. And, unlike most peoples of antiquity, they regarded the realm of the dead not merely as the abode of the shades, but as a dismal region where the souls of the departed, enveloped in black clouds, eternally mourn the irretrievability of life. If what lay in store for them in the end was the terror of annihilation, they should at least not delude themselves about their fate. And since they could not revenge themselves upon the immortals for having laid the sentence of death upon man, they vented their cruelty on the creatures of these immortals. What an extraordinary contrast to the preparation for death of the later Roman Christians! But whether we struggle violently against death or merely sink into it as though it were a never-ending swoon, the reason is the same. It is because death is incomprehensible to us. The manner in which we may meet it cannot alter in any way its incomprehensibility.

The Etruscans apparently tried to rebel against the gods in other ways as well. They continually and deliberately violated the laws of the gods, disregarding all the laws of decency and all the prejudices of convention, such as the notion that courage is better than cowardice, or chastity preferable to debauchery. It is, therefore, quite possible that they practiced in those ancient times what today we call nihilism. But certainly they did not, like us, do so because their faith was so weak; they simply had no illusion whatsoever.

This is one of the few characteristics of the Etruscans we have any knowledge of or, at least, may surmise in them. Otherwise, we scarcely know them. Even their language has remained puzzling to us, and nothing further of any real significance will ever be discovered. They will probably always be removed from us in that realm of the dead which, when they were still alive, held such terror for them. If ever they were to emerge more clearly, it would probably not be they we would see, but their ghosts; chieftains in helmets like the caps of gigantic mushrooms, phantoms in the purple shadows of the laurel groves, spirits on bronze-studded war chariots, disembodied presences clad in effeminate garments, reclining beneath the gray olive trees of the Romagna. For they continue forever to haunt the destiny and history of Rome. Held in check for centuries by the valor and might of the Latins, they yet continually break out in all of their destructiveness, not only in the Romans and the Italians, but in all peoples in the hour of their defeat.

Like Parnassus, the Capitoline had—and still has—two summits. As one mounts the shallow steps, the so-called Cordonata, to the Capitol piazza, the peak dedicated to Jupiter is on the right, the other, sacred to Juno, is on the left. Crowning the summits, high up in the sparkling sunlight, there were once two quiet groves of trees with thick, luxuriant foliage. They were far more beautiful than the later temples; and here, even in very ancient times, the two deities were worshiped. The depression now occupied by the Capitol square was called "the place between the groves." At that time the valley of the Forum was still swampland. Most of the surrounding hills were covered with woods in which wild animals roamed at will, and the settlement on the Palatine, the Roma Quadrata, was still so small that all of its citizens could be summoned from the fields with a horn sounded from the ramparts.

O happy days of long ago when the city was still young! O early, rural Rome! Your sons, a sturdy race of peasant warriors, tilled their own ancestral soil; with their own hands, they yoked the oxen, and when the evening sun cast long shadows from the hills, they bore home on their own shoulders the wood from the forest. Food was simple, clothing plain, and people still honored the gods, the children their parents and the woman the man. Women did not paint their faces, nor did married people break their vows; friend did not betray friend. But when, on the pretext that all this was too rustic, too coarse, too old-fashioned, they strove to make everything bigger and better, their lives at once began to deteriorate. The more the nation's power grew the more did its inner force diminish. The talons of the legions' eagles might stretch to the borders of Latium, might hold all of Italy in their grasp, might reach out toward the ends of the earth; the city which had been built of clay and brick might clothe itself in gilded stone; the peaks of the Capitol might bristle with temples and pillars of Pentelic marble, with triumphal arches and bronze chariots with effigies of its own and conquered gods, with statues stolen from Greece, with the captured banners of foreign peoples and with countless trophies; but the moral decency, the strength of mind and of spirit, in short, the very qualities that had enabled the Romans to build up their vast empire were destroyed by the vastness and the might of their own creation. The city and its empire went down before the assault of the Christian faith which was as strong as the Roman faith once had been, and before the attacks of the tribes of the north who were still young, as the early Romans. The Capitoline temples fell into ruins and rubble. So also did the chapels of the minor gods, the citadel and small roofs over the votive offerings, the pillars of Duilius ornamented with the prows of ships, and the gilded horsemen of Metellus; the monuments of fame and the symbols of might, all went down into the dust, as did Rome's glory itself. And where, long ages before, animals had grazed, goats were grazing again.

There were, to be sure, a few noble hearts, even in Christian Rome, who did not wish to see the sacred hill defiled. Certain noble families, such as the Frangipani, who had settled not only on the hill itself, but down along the side to the Forum and even as far as the Colosseum, were forced to remove themselves and their fortifications. The hill was restored to the Senate and not only adorned with new palaces, but fortified with towers and provided with a sanctuary, a church called the "Altar of Heaven," which was dedicated to the One God. But what we admire on the Capitol today is no longer its true greatness, but only the shadow of it, a mosaic of laboriously excavated and accumulated remains, an image of the majestic glory of the past put together by the unworthy descendants of its great creators.

If one were to draw a line through the hill from east to west, one would divide into two parts not only the city of Rome itself, but the Italian peninsula and the entire Mediterranean area as well. The northern part is filled with the busy life of the present; the southern part, mourning amid its ruins, seems still to cling to the fruitless memories of an irretrievable past. It is as though, in the north, too little faith in heaven had destroyed a higher world; in the south too much faith had destroyed a lower. To the north, even the most venerated vestiges of early Christianity have been buried beneath the edifices of modern times, while to the south, the remains of antiquity still lie exposed, as though nothing living had ever dared to settle again where the blood of the first martyrs was shed; as though no one had been able to clear away the rubble which was all that remained of the palaces of their persecutors. Melancholy, oppression, resignation brood over the Aventine, the Via Latina, the Circus of Maxentius; misery, poverty, and dirt nest among the stones that witnessed the sufferings of the martyrs.

Depressing as is this world of wreckage within the walls of

Rome, the scene outside in the melancholy of the Campagna is even more mournful. The Appian Way is the most famous of the grave-lined streets which lead to this realm of the dead. And there are graves not only along the streets above ground, but also along those below. The streets below are, of course, the passages of the catacombs which, particularly in southern Rome, run all through the ground, and their walls are composed entirely of tombs.

The original name of the catacombs—we are following the account of Carlo Cecchelli, Professor of Christian Archaeology at the University of Rome—was *coemeteria,* that is, sleeping places. They were so called because the bodies of Christians who had died were supposed to be those not of dead but of sleeping men who were waiting to be awakened for the resurrection. In the beginning, the word *catacumbae* itself was used only to designate a particular locality outside the walls of Rome, and only later was extended to include all the subterranean graveyards. The actual place called "*ad catacumbas*" was near the church of St. Sebastian. The Appian Way passed through certain hollows in the ground which, because their shape suggested the hull of a boat, were called *cymbae,* and this word was combined with the Greek *kata,* meaning "down," to form *catacumbae.* "*Ad catacumbas,*" therefore, meant "near the nether hollows." Many pagan graves were there, and it was only later that the spot became a Christian burial ground.

As a rule, in ancient times, the dead were buried in chambers, passages, or vaults, which had been hewn out of the rock. Sometimes the urns with the ashes were placed in the so-called *columbaria,* which contained a large number of niches. Sometimes, as in the case of the Christians, the bodies were not cremated, but were laid in sarcophagi, or beneath so-called pseudosarcophagi, which consisted of rectangular or rounded niches hewn in the tuff wall above the real graves.

The practice of building long, narrow passages was finally adopted in the Roman catacombs, probably owing to lack of space. The boundaries of the burial places were carefully marked with stones and no overlapping was permitted even under the ground. And as the number of the faithful who had to be interred was constantly growing, it was soon necessary to do more digging down below. Here the soft tuff or sandstone of which the ground was composed facilitated the task of the workmen. But of even more assistance were the passages already hewn out for quarries in the rock underlying the tuff. Space was never wasted, and almost always the passages laid out were the long and narrow kind, the so-called *cryptae* which were scarcely higher than a man. When a passage was no longer big enough it was deepened so that the oldest graves were always up close to the ceiling. When it became impossible to deepen a passage, other passages were dug beneath it. Later, in place of the passages with their rows of graves, the so-called *cubicula*, or little chambers, were cut out, as well as sizable burial vaults for entire families or for persons who wished to be buried together.

There were no catacombs in the earliest period of Christianity. The first of them were probably built at the end of the first century and the beginning of the second. These early catacombs, however, consisted only of small groups of passages and it is quite evident that some were isolated vaults which were later connected. Eventually all the various sections dating from widely different periods were linked up. In the process the passages were considerably widened and whole basilicas were constructed under the ground. By the fourth century a great deal of work had been done which had so altered the aspect of the structures that they had become gigantic, subterranean necropolises. But the following centuries added little to them and most of the catacombs were entirely forgotten.

It was not until the sixteenth century that subterranean Rome was rediscovered by Antonio Bosio, the "Columbus of the catacombs." His work was carried on by a long series of men, among them Giuseppe Marchi. But the most outstanding achievements were those of de Rossi who, during the second half of the nineteenth century, rediscovered the so-called *cubiculum pontificum*, the papal vault containing the tombs of Anteros, Fabianus, Lucius, Eutychianus, and nine other popes.

After tracing the historical background, Cecchelli then proceeds to describe the individual sections of subterranean Rome. From among these descriptions we shall single out that of the Praetextatus *coemeterium*. For it was through the maze of passages in these catacombs that Jessiersky tried to escape his pursuers—not only Count Luna, but also the police.

It is quite evident that his original intention was to make them think that he had lost his way and had died. His plan was to come out at a different place from the one at which he had entered, to board a ship, and turn his back on Europe. It may be assumed that it was the disappearance of the two French priests, which he must have read about months before in some paper, that had given him the idea. Otherwise it would be very difficult to explain why he should have gone into the scarcely opened Praetextatus catacombs at all, and particularly without a guide.

Cecchelli describes the *coemeterium* of Praetextatus as follows:

This burial place is situated at the fork between the Via Appia Pignatelli and Via Appia Antica. It was probably part of the estate of Herodes Atticus, a famous financier of antiquity, and his wife, Annia Regilla. In one of the oldest sections of the catacombs there is a cubiculum with an unusual picture of Christ receiving the crown of thorns, and not far from it a Greek epitaph bearing the name of Urania, daughter of Herodes. The latter name, however, probably refers not to the financier himself, but to one of his manumitted slaves, who assumed the name of his master in gratitude for his freedom. In the crypt are two frescoes, one of which represents Christ and the Good Samaritan, the other the Road to Emmaus.

Very ancient also is a somewhat wider passage, called the Spelunta Magna. In this section, where the martyrs Januarius, Cyrinus, Felicissimus, and Agapetus are buried, there is also a niche-shaped room with pillars and marble slabs where the faithful used to gather. A lower story containing portrayals of scenes from the pagan cults of Attis and Sabazios does not belong to the catacombs of Praetextatus. It was originally a separate crypt and at a later time the catacombs, quite by chance, were built alongside of it.

These catacombs, then, are almost entirely unexplored.

It must have been that very fact that caused the two French priests to enter the subterranean passages from Sant'Urbano. Undoubtedly they would not have been permitted to embark on an exploring expedition had they gone in at one of the official entrances. In Sant'Urbano, however, the custodian had no means of stopping them.

Originally, the church of Sant'Urbano was, according to some, an ancient mausoleum dating from the time of the Antonines; according to others, part of the villa of Herodes Atticus. It is situated several hundred feet to the east of the Appian Way and looks like a little temple. The portico supported by marble pillars has recently been uncovered, after being for a long time walled up with bricks. The church faces to the east, and opening out at its feet is the shallow Almo valley, where Egeria is said to have had her grottos and sacred grove.

Before the time of the Roman Republic, her grottos and grove were on the banks of Lake Nemi. It may be conjectured that the two sanctuaries "accompanied" the settlers on their wanderings from there to Rome in much the same way the oracle of the tree of Dodona—from the rustling of whose foliage it was believed one could foretell the future—"accompanied" the Greeks on their journey southward. Whenever they came to a new place, they would search for a new Dodonean Oak resembling the old one that had been left behind. In this same way, the grottos and the grove of Egeria, the nymph, traveled with the Latin tribes from Lake Nemi to Rome. The people wanted them always near because they played an important part in their cult and they could not very well make the long pilgrimage back into the Alban mountains to visit the sanctuaries.

Long ages ago, King Numa Pompilius is said to have often met the nymph in the grove of evergreen oaks, and on one of these occasions, they were united in marriage. In reality, however, this was not the marriage of a simple ruler with a creature of fable, but the mystic union of a so-called priest-king with a priestess of the springs. Those legendary nuptials were reenacted every year, perhaps to fructify and water the land. Surely the grove where those rites were celebrated was not, as it is today, a clump of pitiful bushes overtowered by a couple of trees, but a beautiful shady spinney. But even today the Valley of the Nymph is not always a desolate place. The broom was in blossom at the time of Jessiersky's visit at Sant'Urbano, and the whole region was filled with the scent of tall grass and wild flowers.

In all probability, Alexander Jessiersky, on his underground excursion, had carried with him the maps of the catacombs drawn up by a certain Casamonte. This was the conclusion the Vienna official, Dr. Julius Gambs, arrived at when, in the course of a careful search of the Strattmann Palace, he happened to glance through the library catalogue. It was not necessary, of course, for this already overworked man to check the catalogue, let alone to examine the books. He did so of his own free will, for he was rather interested in so-called erotic literature, and he took this opportunity to see if he could find anything of this nature in the Strattmann Palace. He found no pornography, but, as he was going over the catalogue, his eye lighted on the heading "Catacombs" which struck him as important from another, more pertinent point of view. Listed under this heading were Casamonte's maps. But when Dr. Gambs went to take out the book, he found that it was no longer there. From this he concluded that Jessiersky must have taken the volume with him. The book, of course, might have got lost in some other way. But this was improbable, for it was the only work on catacombs in the library, and when, from the same house, a book about the Roman catacombs disappears, and a man into them, it stands to reason that they probably disappeared together.

Whereas most public servants are merely indolent, Dr. Gambs was made up of a mixture of indolence and intelligence; and the latter won the day in the present instance. He betook himself to the National Library and asked for a copy of Casamonte's map book.

The work, dedicated to a Cardinal Chigi, had been published in 1721 in Rome. Following the Latin dedication there was a lengthy introduction written in Italian; the maps, when unfolded, were two or three feet square, while the leather-bound book itself was only eleven by twelve inches in size. A person visiting the catacombs could conveniently carry the book in his coat pocket.

Dr. Gambs made no attempt to study the dedication in Latin, which he had all but forgotten, or the introduction in Italian, of which he knew not a word. He proceeded at once to the maps themselves which showed the most important sections of the catacombs and were ornamented with pictures of the gods of the underworld, of Hades and of Tartarus, and of the moon goddesses, Hecate, Persephone, and Alcestis. The legends were again in Italian, but, after a short time, Dr. Gambs was able to discover that a connection had been indicated between the Praetextatus and the St. Sebastian catacombs. Many of the other catacombs, however, were also linked up, and to what extent these connections were actual and to what extent hypothetical, Gambs could not, of course, determine. For old maps rarely differentiate between the hypothetical and the actual. But, for the moment, at least, these distinctions did not interest him. It was enough for him that Jessiersky, too, might have seen the connection marked down there between the Praetextatus and the St. Sebastian catacombs. If he had, he might either have tried to get out at once through the main entrance to the Praetextatus catacombs, which is situated near Sant'Urbano in a sand pit, or he might have gone first over into the St. Sebastian catacombs and then have attempted to find his way out somewhere near the Via Ardeatina, or even through the catacombs of St. Nereus and Achilles.

It would have been better, of course, if, during his last days in Rome, Jessiersky had tried to hunt up maps more up-to-date than those of Casamonte. But he seemed to have been misled by the clarity of the Casamonte maps, assuming them to be as correct as they were clear, and to have consulted no other books.

Dr. Gambs might well have been satisfied to leave the matter there. But having, for once, bestirred himself, he was not satisfied to drop it at this stage. It occurred to him that Jessiersky, knowing that he was being pursued, could hardly have hoped to escape his pursuers on the *Aosta*, on which he had booked passage in his own name. A cable to the police of Buenos Aires asking them to arrest a certain Herr Alexander Jessiersky, who had officially died in the catacombs, but who might conceivably have gone ashore in Argentina, would have sufficed to bring all his plans to nothing. It was most likely, then, that his booking passage on the *Aosta* had only been a maneuver to put off his pursuers, and that Jessiersky had planned to escape to safety by another ship and under another name. If such a plan failed, there should be some record of a berth which, engaged about that time aboard another ship for a passenger of another name, had not been occupied. And Dr. Gambs, in fact, discovered that a ticket had been purchased for the *Independence*, which had sailed from Genoa for New York on May 12th, for a man with the rather odd name of Friedlichkeit, apparently a German, whose ticket had never been turned in.

Seldom, if ever, does it happen that a paid passage remains unused, that it is not canceled in time. But the place on the *Independence* had not been occupied and from this it was to be concluded that, while the *Aosta* ticket was not supposed to have been turned in, it had not been possible to turn in the *Independence* ticket. What is more, it turned out that no Herr Friedlichkeit existed or had ever existed. Friedlichkeit's cabin had, in reality, been engaged by Jessiersky for himself under a false name and with a forged passport which probably had been procured in Munich. And if ever Jessiersky had got out of the catacombs, he would have gone not to Naples, but to Genoa, and would have left Europe not on the *Aosta*, but on the *Independence*.

But he had been unable to carry out his plan, and instead of sailing the ocean, he had had to wade through the waters of the Lethe. And a happening which he had meant only to simulate had actually taken place. The details of his death, of course, could not be reported. But they were of no great importance to the authorities; for them it was enough to know that Jessiersky had ceased to exist.

Chapter 12

Jessiersky had soon discovered that Casamonte's maps, while not precisely inaccurate, were incomplete to the point of misguiding him. Where, for example, the maps showed one passage branching off from another, there were often two or even three others, and in places where they indicated only one, or at most two stories, there were frequently many more, one above another. Jessiersky had thought that, in general, he would be able to walk along on one level, but he found before long that he had to deal with three dimensions. One level rose up above another, and the whole interior of the earth seemed riddled with tunnels and cavities, like a honeycomb or sponge, so that it would have required descriptive geometry to give the true picture. The maps were not actual representations; they were merely simplified diagrams. Details were sacrificed for the sake of overall clarity. Moreover, the maps were drawn on a small scale so that large areas could be shown on a single page and give the impression of vastness. The final result was not so much a distortion as a modification of reality.

Cardinal Chigi, however, may very well have been pleased with them. Seated at the desk in his palace, leafing through the expensively bound copy which had just been handed to him, he undoubtedly noted with satisfaction that the dedication composed in Latin distichs contained a reference to the supposed descent of Chigi from a patrician *gens*. To Casamonte, who stood most respectfully behind his chair, anxiously observing the effect of his poetical points upon this prince of the church, the cardinal may well have made the comment, which was as indulgent as it was ambiguous, that the cartographer's venture into the domain of poetry had been decidedly successful. Unfortunately, however, Casamonte's poetry had carried over into the maps. For to leave out the unessential is of the essence of poetry. And in the dedication, Casamonte had not only failed to mention that the patrician Chigis, who claimed to be relatives of the Juliuses and Flaviuses, were really descended from an obscure and quite ordinary banker; but also suppressed everything on the maps that might have marred the general effect of the beautifully ornamented pages. To the cardinal, in his castle with its broad vista, this was not in the least disturbing. He had never set foot into the underworld of Rome, except once, or perhaps twice, when a service had been held in the tomb chapel of St. Cecilia. But to a man who was about to lose his way in the catacombs, those beautiful pages were profoundly disturbing, and Alexander Jessiersky cursed the tendency of the world to color everything to suit its taste and needs. He himself, of course, had once been in favor of this kind of coloring. But now he was in favor of it no longer.

He was now willing to admit, however, that his attempt to flee from the moon through the catacombs, without any previous reconnoitering, had been rank foolishness. For he realized that he had greatly underestimated the difficulty and the danger of the undertaking. He had supposed that in picking his way through passages that had been laid out not by nature but by man, he would encounter no insurmountable obstacles. But he had forgotten that the catacombs, unlike a house that is built by a few men, had been the work of thousands, perhaps tens of thousands.

When Jessiersky saw that he had little chance of reaching the main entrance to the Praetextatus Catacombs in the sand pit and none at all of finding the spot on the other side of the Via Ardeatina where he had hoped to get back above ground, he decided to return to Sant'Urbano and give up his attempt to put the moon off the track, at least for the time being. He came to this decision fairly soon, for his transatlantic voyage was very much on his mind. By now Achtner would surely have been found, and the investigation of his death would soon be completed. And when, as would undoubtedly be the case, it was proved that he, Jessiersky, had been the murderer, and when later on he was also charged with the shooting of Eisl and the murder of Spinette, the Austrian police would not be long in requesting the Italian authorities to hunt down the fugitive and arrest him. Under no circumstances, therefore, must he miss the *Independence*; and he now felt no further desire to go in for extensive explorations under the earth, even if he had to put up with the moon for a while longer. The opportunity to get rid of it would present itself later on.

But this attempt to beat the moon with its own weapons was to result only in the moon's beating Jessiersky with his. For when he tried to return to Sant'Urbano, he could no longer find his way back from the shadowed side of the earth, out of the underworld of the moon, to the light world of the sun.

After the first two days, although he had eaten very sparingly of his small supply of food, he had nothing left to eat, and he began to be tormented by a frightful thirst. On the third day—he still kept track of the time by his watch—he realized that he could no longer get to the *Independence*. But was it not possible, he wondered, if he were able to stay down here forever, that he might yet be able to put the moon off the scent? For down here the moon could no longer do him any harm.

He would sink down exhausted and lean back against a wall, or he would lie down in the dust and sleep. In between times, he went on groping his way along in the darkness because he wanted to save his candles. Then too, he thought, without them he could more easily discover the light shafts which were supposed to have been cut through in various places, the so-called *luminaria*. He had heard that most of these openings had become blocked up and that some of them had been reduced to the merest crack. But so far he had not come upon any. Perhaps also it had been moonless night up there when he groped past the shafts, and this was a new prank of the moon to prevent him from finding them.

Then he began to be afraid that he might bump into the dead bodies of the two priests in the darkness, and he felt his way more slowly, walking on the tips of his toes like a moonstruck dog. But then it occurred to him that he would be warned of their presence well in advance by the odor of decay. Or had they become mummies now, indistinguishable from the others which, here and there, had fallen out of the tombs or had been dragged out, far back in the past, by plundering barbarians? He frequently had the feeling that he was brushing against mummies, and once something stuck to the sole of his shoe like a spur. When he lit a candle, he saw that he had stepped squarely into the middle of a lower jawbone which had been lying in the passage and which now spanned the heel of his shoe as neatly as the clasp of a spur.

The suitcase and the coat, even the hat, he had lost long before. From time to time bats would sweep past him, grazing him with their wings. But by the time he had struck a light in order to try to follow them to their exit, they would already have disappeared. He pictured to himself the openings through which they flew out into the open air. Up on the plain, when they fluttered out blindly in swarms, it must look as though an oil volcano were shooting up, in a black spray, a mass of rippling black clouds. Real volcanoes, thought Jessiersky, now becoming delirious, shot up jets of fire from an underworld river called Pyriphlegethon. But probably it had a tributary composed of bats, and the bats were being shot up into the air by the oil volcanoes.

It was about the eighth or ninth day that he suddenly saw light. At first he thought that he had at last come upon a shaft. Then he thought someone had come to look for him. But when he saw two priests coming toward him, who stopped and spoke to him in French, he knew that they must be the two French priests who had died in the catacombs.

One of them was slender, well-proportioned, aristocratic in his bearing and also somewhat younger than his companion who was short and stocky and had a rather crafty expression on his face. With a sanctimonious air, he kept averting his eyes from Jessiersky, who stood rooted to the spot.

At last he found his voice. "So you are alive?" he cried out. "I don't know what to think! I told the man up there that I was coming down here to look for you, but that was only a pretext! In reality—please forgive me—I never doubted for a moment that you were dead."

The priests looked at him for a while in silence, then the slender one said: "Monsieur de Jessiersky, you have spoken only a few words to us. Nevertheless, we notice with regret that your French is not of the best. You should have availed yourself of the opportunity to learn it better from your late father."

"Do you think so?" asked Jessiersky, who was much too confused to be surprised that they should know not only about him but also about his father. "Yes, yes, that's quite possible. But tell me, *are* you dead, or aren't you?"

"If we were," said the short one after a long silence, "you would at least have to believe in immortality. Isn't that true?"

"Do you think so?"

"Certainly."

"But why? Or if you are still alive, explain to me at least what you've been living on all this time. I, too, brought along a small supply, but I finished it up long ago, and I am starving. You must have dragged in whole mountains of provisions to be standing there alive before me now. And why did you come down here in the first place? Were you really interested in the catacombs, or were you simply trying—tell me honestly—to get away from the moon?"

"The moon," said the slender one, poking with the tip of his toe the remains of a mummy which was lying in the dust. "You can neither escape from the moon nor not escape from it. The moon is the symbol of illusion, the sign of the uncertainty under which we exist."

"Why can't you escape from the moon?" cried Jessiersky. "I myself almost escaped from it!"

"But only almost!"

"Ah, now I see that you *are* dead," said Jessiersky. "But you are ashamed of having died. For why else would you answer me so evasively? That also explains why you apparently don't want to tell me that I, too, am already dead."

"So you think," inquired the short priest, "that you yourself are no longer among the living?"

"Certainly."

"Then you do believe in immortality after all?"

"No," said Jessiersky, "obviously I do not believe in it. For how could we be talking about our death—although, come to think of it, we *would* have to be immortal to talk about it after it had taken place. But perhaps you can at least explain death to me. As you can see, I hadn't even noticed that I was dead. Is it possible that you, too, haven't noticed yet that you are dead?"

"I really don't know why you want to know that," said the slender priest. "For, after all, everything is just what we think it is, what we take it to be. And the same applies to man and his situation. Considered from the standpoint of the body, he is, of course, mortal. But when you consider him from the point of view of his soul, he can only be immortal. For the soul is the nonmortal aspect of man, and what is not physical does not die. Therefore one and the same being, man, is both mortal and immortal."

Jessiersky made a wry face. "That sort of immortality," he said, "would give me little pleasure."

"But there is no other."

"Quite frankly, it's too abstract for me."

"Unfortunately, I can't oblige you with a more concrete variety. For our only organ for existence, our only connection with the world is our body. It sinks into the tangible, as the so-called 'foot' of a shell sinks into the mud, and if we lose it, we are confined to the abstract. To make it more palatable to you, I would have to express myself more poetically."

"How, may I ask?"

"By trying to use allegories. I might, for example, do something with the idea that one returns in death to the place of one's birth. In that event, we, my companion and I, would return to France, because all of our forebears lived there, and you, Monsieur de Jessiersky, would return to Galicia, to Poland...."

"To Poland?" exclaimed Jessiersky, surprised that even the most private thoughts of his youth seemed to be known to this priest. "To Poland, you say? But what would I do in Poland, now that everything has been confiscated there! Even in Bohemia my late wife's two ..."

"Oh, among the dead nothing is confiscated," said the slender priest, "and particularly not among dead Poles. It is conceivable that Germans and Czechs might still take things away from one another in death, but under no circumstances would anything like that happen in Poland. The nobility there are still happily ensconced on their estates, even though they might have squandered them away long ago, and they are being waited on by all the people who are not nobles. Among the dead any attempt to introduce social reforms would be quite hopeless. Even those who would benefit, reject them here, as of course, do those who wouldn't...."

"I, too," said Jessiersky, "have always imagined it to be like that, or very much like that. Isn't that strange?"

"No, not at all," returned the slender priest. "For, although it is reactionary, or perhaps just because it is reactionary, it fits very well into the picture we have of death. You have no idea how extremely reactionary our pictures of death are! But however that may be, I can very well imagine that you too, when you die, instead of being taken to the cemetery in a hearse, will be carried in a sleigh to Poland...."

"But that's extraordinary," cried Jessiersky, "really too extraordinary that you should happen to mention the sleigh! Although, unfortunately, I am convinced that no sleigh will ever carry *me* to Poland. There was one for my poor father, but there will be no sleigh for me."

"Oh, yes, oh, yes," said the priest reassuringly. "For you, too. To Poland. A sleigh, drawn by two tall half-breeds with ornamented harnesses and bells on the headstalls. To Wiazownika or Marianowka, whichever you please. Into a kind of Jessiersky heaven. You have earned it at long last by your little episodes with Spinette and Eisl and Achtner, though originally you would never have thought of ..."

"But, good heavens," cried Jessiersky aghast. "Do you know all about that too? How can you possibly know?"

"Know?" replied the priest. "I don't know it. I am just making up a story about your life and your death. I am only expressing myself poetically. For none of this down below here is real. It's all an invented immortality, nothing more…."

"Invented?"

"Yes, of course."

"But then what's the use of it?"

"Of what?"

"Of immortality?"

"It has no use," replied the priest. "None. For if a living thing dies, it passes from one situation in which it still is into another in which it no longer is. And once you no longer are, how can you possibly have anything? Then you neither are anything nor have anything. You have simply become nothing and have ceased to be."

"And so there really is no immortality?"

"No. It exists, but only insofar as the nothing you have entered into exists, which is to say that even that which no longer is, still is. If it had never been, it certainly would no longer be. But because it was, it still is. Only that which no longer is can no longer be understood in terms of what still is. We can only infer that this is so, but it is impossible for us, beyond the abyss of death, to picture it."

"I heartily agree," said Jessiersky. "It's quite impossible to picture it, quite futile to try to imagine the so-called life of the dead."

"And what is more," continued the priest, "we are also misled by the blank nothingness itself, by what has never been and never will be, by negation itself. But nevertheless, I can assure you we will certainly not fall victim to it. For since we once have been, we are. That is to say, we shall never cease to be. We are forever. For through our own being, we also share in the Divine Being: and

God, although He is not the world that is (or rather just because He is not the world that He created and which passes, because He is its opposite, the uncreated which, therefore, cannot pass) is everlasting and immutable—like ourselves."

"You know," said Jessiersky after a pause, "I would much prefer it if it weren't such a complicated business where something that is 'is not' and something that is not 'is.' If it only had some connection with the immortality of the soul as it used to be and as we learned it. Isn't the soul per se immortal? Is it really only man?"

"Yes, only man," replied the slender priest. "Nothing but man—man as God sees him."

"And God Himself?" inquired Jessiersky, "What is God?"

"Again just man as he sees himself," replied the priest.

"Is that so!" cried Jessiersky. "That never would have occurred to me!"

"But that's how it is, or at least more or less how it is," said the stocky priest. As he spoke he looked off to the side.

"Do you think so?" asked Jessiersky. "I know you are only trying to break it to me gently that there is no such thing as a life after death. For if one could die without passing away, one would not have to be born in order to be. But one thing I really don't understand. If we no longer exist after we die, if everything is really over, why are we so afraid of death? I myself, at least, have been afraid of it all my life. I was afraid that a single moment might take me away, far away from everything familiar...."

"And quite rightly so," said the short priest. "For without fear of death you would have been so careless that you would have been killed even as a child. But are you afraid of it now—of death?"

"Frankly, I am too exhausted to be very much afraid of anything."

"Now, you see! You're afraid only of nothingness. But there

really isn't much more to death. Although it is a most common occurrence, it is vastly overestimated. For not only every human being, but every dog, every fly must eventually give up the ghost. If there were really anything else to dying, the cattle, who never die a natural death but are always slaughtered, ought to be given a score of medals, like generals. And think of how unimportant the death of creatures that died a hundred or only fifty years ago has become!"

"But I am still living," said Jessiersky. "I did not live fifty or a hundred years ago and so I am tremendously interested in knowing whether I am dying, which, by the way, I shall certainly do if you don't quickly give me something out of that food supply of yours which has kept you so fresh. For, after all, I've been down here for eight days and …"

"Fourteen days," corrected the slender priest, and turning to the short priest he said: "Give Monsieur de Jessiersky something to eat. Do you really regret," he asked, again addressing Jessiersky, "your evil deeds?"

"I suppose so," said Jessiersky. "But I myself was misled. Do hurry up and give me something to eat!"

Then the stocky priest took a box out of his pocket and with a quick, deft movement, so that Jessiersky could not see what it was, he took something white out of the box and popped it into Jessiersky's mouth. As he did so he moved his lips almost soundlessly.

The white object tasted of nothing. "What was that?" asked Jessiersky.

"Nothing, nothing," the slender priest said.

"Is that all?" cried Jessiersky seeing that the short man had put away the box.

"Yes," said the slender priest.

"What, is that all I'm going to get?"

"You couldn't stand any more because you haven't eaten for so long."

"But how about something to drink?" inquired Jessiersky, forcing himself to be agreeable. "Something out of a flask."

"Are you perhaps related to the Piast kings? I'd never heard that you were!"

"What do you mean, to the Piast kings?"

"Or perhaps to the Jagellon kings? But we really didn't come to meet you in order to talk about all kinds of things about which we really know nothing ourselves. Especially …"

"Did you come to meet me?"

"Yes."

"So you knew I would come?"

"Yes, of course. That is why we've been wandering about down here for months."

"That is why?" cried Jessiersky. "What do you mean by that?"

"Just that you might have made an effort not to come entirely unprepared yourself. You haven't even got your coat with you any longer."

"My coat? Why yes … I seem to have lost it. But dragging it around all these days, you know … and then I really don't need it any more. It may be a little damp here, but it's quite warm, and …"

"Soon it will become quite cold."

"Cold?"

"Yes, cold."

"Why?"

"There is snow on the ground after all."

"But how does that happen? Now, in May?"

"In May you think?"

"Yes, and in Italy too!"

"Oh, come along!" said the slender priest, and he and the

shorter man took Jessiersky between them, seized him by the arms, and led him away.

"Where are we going so suddenly?" cried Jessiersky.

"Up, of course! You talk a great deal and ask a good many questions in your bad French!"

They had gone only a few steps when the passage came to an end. Light came flooding in. The priests led Jessiersky across a heap of rubble of mummy fragments, into the open.

"How rude the fellows have become all of a sudden," said Jessiersky to himself. "I would as soon trust the care of my soul to the horns of the moon as to these two horns of salvation!"

"Come, come!" shouted the priests, dragging him along.

"You act as though you were taking me to the scaffold!" protested Jessiersky.

"Which is where you really belong!"

But by that time they were already up above. They were in the midst of a snowy plain and not far away a sleigh was waiting.

But this can't be the Roman plain, thought Jessiersky. How far the catacombs extend under the ground! Where can I be?

The priests had suddenly vanished, and Jessiersky, while he was glad to be rid of them, felt utterly at a loss. He began walking toward the sleigh. Draped over the back of the carriage was a lap robe of fox fur, and the horses, obviously tall half-breeds, gaily shook their heads with the ornamented, jingling harness.

Two people in fur coats were seated on the box. One of them immediately jumped down and ran toward Jessiersky. He took off his fur coat and put it around Jessiersky's shoulders.

Jessiersky saw that the man was wearing livery. "Where do you come from?" he asked. "Where am I? Why is there snow? Whose sleigh is that?"

To all these questions the man, who had blunt features, black hair, and extraordinarily coarse hands, replied merely: "Maria-nowka."

Then Jessiersky knew that he was dead.

"Well, well," he thought, swallowing hard, "so one does die after all. You refuse to believe that someday you will die. But then you die and you don't even notice it. And the fact that you don't is the best thing about dying."

As he walked along, he realized that the Jezierskijs had sent the sleigh for him, after all. It had come from the Jezierskijs themselves, not from the Raczynskis or the Szoldrskis. For the Jezierskijs were living in Marianowka, even though they had squandered it away. They were still in Marianowka and Wiazownika, and they had sent the sleigh for him, as they had sent it for his father, Adam Jessiersky.

After he had climbed onto the sleigh, he again asked some questions of the man who had put the fur coat around him and of the other man who had remained on the box. But they answered him in a language that he did not understand. Probably it was Polish. He tried once more in French, but again they replied in Polish. Perhaps Polish was the language of the dead, or, perhaps, being servants, they spoke Ruthenian. But he could not understand that either.

As he was settling back on the fox-fur robe, the liveried man, who was apparently a footman, spread over his knees a second lap robe, which had been folded up on the floor of the sleigh. Then he leaped up onto the box beside the coachman. The horses began to pull, and at once the sleigh was skimming across the snow with the speed of lightning.

The bells were jingling, and the fox tails, which were sewn onto the sleigh robe, were fluttering in the icy wind. Then from the distance came music. Jessiersky noticed that it was a Fantaisie by

Chopin.... Hadn't Chopin also provided the music for Adam Jessiersky's ride with the Uhlan squadrons? This time he was playing the Fantaisie in F minor. He kept playing it over and over, for by modern standards he did not play particularly well—apparently he was trying to improve his playing by repetition.... And they rode on beneath a sky holding the threat of snow, but from which no snow fell, over rolling hills and endless plains covered with old snow; and through gloomy woods and again over plains and through more woods which became darker and darker as night fell. The howling of wolves became mingled with the Chopin music as they dashed on through the icy night. "Perhaps," thought Jessiersky, recalling what the slender priest had said, "perhaps this is only the poetic embellishment of death. The snow over which we are riding is not real snow, but the Cocytus; the coachman, if one looks closely, will turn out to be Charon, and the sleigh, his skiff. Perhaps all this, because it is only an embellishment of horror, will soon pass and give place to utter nothingness...." But nothing passed. Everything persisted. Finally lights appeared, dogs barked, and the sleigh swung around and drew up in front of a lighted house.

This must be Marianowka.... But Alexander Jessiersky had no time to look at it. Scarcely had the sleigh stopped under the portico, which was supported by white wooden pillars, when the door of the house flew open. Servants with lanterns came rushing out, helped him from the sleigh, and hustled him into the house. A crowd of people converged upon him from many lighted rooms and spoke to him in French.

In their midst, Alexander Jessiersky recognized his father.

"Well, my boy," cried Adam Jessiersky, "Here you are! I mean you are really here! For this, heaven knows, you have Luna and Spinette to thank and the two simpletons from Zinkeneck who passed through here and told us about you. Otherwise we might have waited for you indefinitely. But now you're here. How goes your French, by the way?"

"*Le Comte de la Lune est ici?*" stammered Alexander Jessiersky.

"*Le Comte de Lune* was not *ici*, but *là*," corrected Adam Jessiersky. "Of course he was *là*, and had been for a long time. Or did you think he wasn't *là*? What an idiot you were! But what luck you've had!" And he slapped him jovially on the back, as an archduke slaps the back of a member of the general staff.

He was not wearing the uniform of the general staff, but a uhlan uniform, such as he had never worn in life. What is more, he was no longer emaciated by cancer, but had regained his former stoutness.

Behind him appeared Witold and Olgerd Jesierskij, Pavel, and the already legendary Alexander, who, as Adam Jessiersky explained, was here only by chance and would soon return to Russia. They all embraced their descendant and kissed him on both cheeks. The Szoldrskis, the Raczynskis, and the Bielskis also came over to speak to him. They were all laughing, not as though he had just died, but as though something extremely amusing had taken place, and they welcomed him heartily.

"Come on in," said Adam Jessiersky, "come on in, you will certainly want to greet the ladies."

But Alexander Jessiersky asked if it were absolutely necessary to do so that evening. He was dead tired from wandering around under the earth and from the long sleigh ride, and he very much needed a shave, as anyone could see. Would it not be possible for him to go right to bed and see the ladies tomorrow. He was utterly exhausted from so many impressions and …

"Come, come!" laughed Adam Jessiersky. "Excuses! Nothing but excuses! What you're really afraid of is suddenly meeting up with Luna, and you think he may possibly be sitting in the parlor making conversation! Isn't that it?"

"But where is he really?"

"He went on, went on long ago! For here is only ..."

"What is it only?"

"Nothing, nothing. Come along now!"

"But wasn't he the moon?"

"Who?"

"This Luna."

"Oh, why should you think that? He was just a starving little sociologist, that's all."

And he drew his son into the big parlor where the ladies were sitting and Alexander Jessiersky had to greet them each in turn. He liked the Bielski girl best of all. She was really charming, and he thought that Pavel Jezierskij had been quite justified in lavishing all that money on her. Wine and liqueurs were passed around and everyone drank his health, and he had to drink everyone's health until he began to feel quite giddy, for he was drinking on an empty stomach. The few canapes served with the wine didn't amount to much. He badly wanted to go to bed. But already someone had sat down at the piano and was playing "La Valse Brune" which gave him quite a turn and everyone laughed. But then other pieces were played and everyone began to dance. Alexander Jessiersky danced with his grandmother and above all with his enchanting great-grandmother. Again and again he tried his skill at six-step waltzes, mazurkas, polkas, and polonaises, and this went on until morning....

"Could this really be the Beyond?" he muttered, confused, exhausted and drunk. "Probably this way of being dead doesn't exist. One simply imagines it. It is only, as the scrawny priest said, decked out more poetically than the real, ordinary way of being dead...."

"Be quiet!" scolded Adam Jessiersky. "You're not supposed to talk like that. You shouldn't cheat yourself of your illusions. Let's simply assume, although it certainly isn't true, that death is just like life, sleep like waking, youth like age, one place like another, and that one never knows exactly where one is…. But day is dawning. It is already stealing through the curtains, as they put it so beautifully in novels. Come, we must really go to bed now. The days have little meaning here; the nights are everything."

With this he put his beautiful beringed hand, which had emerged from the narrow sleeve of his tunic, around his son's shoulder, and, yawning, began to mount the stairs leading to the bedrooms. The upper hall, lighted by a few candles, was adorned in the strangest fashion. The walls were entirely papered with faded, brownish photographs. There were hundreds, perhaps thousands of them. They covered the entire hallway like fish scales. What they represented, Alexander Jessiersky could not exactly see in the dim light. They seemed to be pictures of men in uniform and in outmoded civilian clothes, of horses, of dogs— long dead, all of them, countless long-forgotten beings.

Two servants were waiting in the hall. Alexander Jessiersky recognized one of them as the man who had put the fur coat around him as he came out of the catacombs, the man in livery with the black hair, the blunt features, and the coarse hands. "He is still on duty," thought Jessiersky. "I should have demanded long hours like that of my own servants! But in eternity …"

"So much work! So many guests!" he muttered, already beginning to speak thickly. But the servant did not seem to understand him. He merely smiled and said a few words to his comrade in a strange language, perhaps it was Ruthenian. In any case Alexander Jessiersky still did not understand the language of the dead. And the two men received him and led him into the bedroom.

As he passed the door, he looked about for his father, but he had already gone. Then Alexander Jessiersky went into the room. The servants undressed him and put him to bed, and the moment he lay down he fell asleep and at last lost consciousness.